DEADLY ILLUSIONS

Chester D. Campbell

To Judy

[signature]

DURBAN HOUSE

DEADLY ILLUSIONS

Copyright ©2005, Chester D. Campbell

All rights reserved. No part of this book may be used or reproduced in any manner whatsoever without the written permission of the Publisher.

Printed in the United States of America.

For information address:
Durban House Publishing Company, Inc.
7502 Greenville Avenue, Suite 500, Dallas, Texas 75231

Library of Congress Cataloging-in-Publication Data
Campbell, Chester D., 1925–

Deadly Illusions / by Chester D. Campbell

Library of Congress Catalog Number: 2004115672

p. cm.

ISBN 1-930754-65-5

First Edition

10 9 8 7 6 5 4 3 2 1

Visit our Web site at
http://www.durbanhouse.com

To Jim Campbell
who never fails to come up with the answer

Other Greg McKenzie Mysteries by Chester D. Campbell:
Secret of the Scroll
Designed to Kill

Acknowledgements

Special thanks to my manuscript critics, members of the Quill & Dagger Writers Guild in Madison, TN — Beth Terrill-Hicks, Richard Emerson, Larry Henry, and Jeannie Arnold. Also thanks to several Metro Nashville Homicide Division officers, including Sgt. R. V. Smith and Detectives E. J. Bernard, Brad Corcoran, Robert Anderson, and Joe Williams. I received valuable input from technical advisor Jim Campbell and a bit of Scottish lore from Robert Bruce Thompson. Bob Middlemiss kept me in focus. And, as always, thanks to Sarah.

1

FOR A GUY WHO'D HAD A MAJOR PROBLEM with much of Metro Nashville's finest a little more than a year ago, I was hardly overjoyed at finding myself in the midst of the department's most tormenting case in years. Okay, maybe not in the midst. I was more like on the periphery, which was still a lot closer than I cared to be.

It happened on one of those spectacular early spring days that could have inspired a poet to grab pen and paper. The sky appeared so blue it dazzled. Early-blooming lilacs spread like a purple haze along the driveway, heavily scenting the nippy morning breeze. Jill and I left home full of anticipation, bound for lunch at Nashville's spectacular Opryworld Hotel. We were meeting a prospect we hoped to make the first major client of McKenzie Investigations.

The gentleman in question, one Jesse Logan by name, awaited us in the spacious Lakeside Lobby on the far side of the sprawling hotel. He stood next to a mammoth fluted column with a Corinthian style capital, although I doubted the good folks from Corinth ever sculpted a stylized guitar on all four sides. Even if I'd not had the benefit of a previous investigative career, Logan would not have been all that difficult to spot among the throng of stockbrokers, analysts and such who had descended on the hotel for a meeting of securities dealers. Logan had told me he would look a little bit like Tiger Woods. In fact, he appeared to be early- to mid-thirties, medium height, trim, dressed in a brown knit shirt and khaki slacks. He didn't share Tiger's tentative grin, but I found him leaning against a tall, leather-adorned bag from which a mob of wood and metal heads protruded.

I approached him with a confident smile. "Mr. Logan?"

He glanced at his watch. "You must be Greg McKenzie. Right on time. Punctuality, I like." Looking across at Jill, he said, "And this would be Mrs. McKenzie?"

It would, indeed. He reached out to take Jill's hand, giving rise to what I called her motherly smile. Though old enough to be a grandmother several times over, she had coal-black hair and an attractive face and figure that made too many people wonder if she might not be my daughter. Happily, she was not. I'd had neither sons nor daughters but one wife for over thirty-five years.

"A pleasure to meet you, Mr. Logan," Jill said.

I shook his hand also, approving of the firm grasp, then noted a set to his jaw that appeared to signal he was not the type who preferred standing around making small talk. "Ready for some lunch?" I asked.

"I sure am. I just got in from playing the Summerhouse Course with a lawyer I'm consulting about our situation. If you don't mind, I'll just bring the bag along and save some time. No telling how long it would take to get to my room and back."

"Amen to that," I said. The Opryworld's room wings wandered off in every conceivable direction from its numerous lobbies and ballrooms and its monstrous areas under glass. "Bring the clubs. There's a good eating place in the Lakeside area."

"Great," he said, smiling broadly. "I'll confess, though, I'm a bit of a stickler when it comes to my menu preferences."

Logan, from Atlanta, had told me on the phone he was southeast regional manager for Leisure Foods Group, which operated a chain of specialty restaurants called King Cole's. That had led me to speculate that he might be a merry old soul. The age category certainly didn't fit.

The hotel's restaurants were a tad pricey, but we were here to impress a prospect. Jill was decked out in a fashionable blue and white outfit and, though I preferred more casual attire, I wore my dark gray suit with the patterned red tie. I would certainly have been impressed were I in Logan's shoes. We escorted him through a brick archway into an area that resembled a tropical garden. Large green plants grew in profusion among pools dotted with dancing water spouts. Off to the right was one of the hotel's half a dozen eating spots, one that resembled a sidewalk café not far from a high waterfall that gushed out of huge manmade rocks. Nearby, a rotating lounge sat like a lily pad on an indoor lake. High above, you could see blue sky through what looked like acres of glass. Now *that* was impressive.

After Jill and I had ordered sandwiches considerably more expensive than McDonald's and Logan had vetoed everything but a fruit plate, I asked him how he'd come to know Metro Detective Phillip Adamson, the officer who had recommended us.

"I got his name from a friend in the Atlanta Police Department. When I talked to Adamson, he said you two had been in business for only a few months. But he pointed out that you were retired from the Air Force Office of Special Investigations and had been an investigator for the DA's office in Nashville. He also told me about the murder case you folks solved down in Florida last fall."

Phil Adamson had become a good friend—one of few in the Metro PD—despite a rocky start nearly a year and a half ago when I had stonewalled him while struggling to track down a group of Palestinians who had kidnapped Jill.

Logan proceeded to explain the problem that plagued him, which involved the King Cole's unit in Hendersonville, a trendy town just across the county line on the northeast side of Nashville. It seemed that several employees, possibly including the manager, were suspected of skimming cash from the operation. The customer base appeared to be holding firm, though gross receipts were sliding down a slippery slope.

"We don't want to get the cops involved and risk a rash of bad publicity," he said. "We're looking for a private detective agency to get a handle on the situation."

The waitress brought our food, and as Logan picked his way through a mound of fruit and cottage cheese, Jill and I dug into sandwiches big enough for King Kong if not King Cole. As we ate, a burly ex-Metro police captain named Haley Edwards waved at me, then took a seat at a nearby table. He was security chief at the hotel. I had met him during my all-too-brief tenure with the District Attorney's office. In light of his own problems with Nashville's police hierarchy, he had readily expressed sympathy for my agonizing plight.

I was well into charting some possible routes the King Cole's investigation might take when I saw Edwards jam a cell phone against his ear. His eyes widened. His face took on a doomsday look. He jumped up from the table, nearly knocked over his chair, and ran for the entrance.

Hearing the clatter and seeing the puzzled look on my face, Logan turned in time to catch a glimpse of the fleeing hotel official. "What the devil was that all about?"

"He's head of Opryworld's security," I said. "From the looks of it, I'd say he has a major problem."

Jill took that as a cue and donned a demure smile. "Why don't we get back to how McKenzie Investigations can help with your problem, Mr. Logan?"

Count on my wife to seize the moment.

"Well, actually, you've pretty well convinced me you're the people to solve our dilemma," he said. He looked across at Jill. "I like the idea of your going in as a hostess to take an inside look at what's happening out there. Tell me a little more about what you have in mind."

"At the moment, I'm just kicking around some ideas," I

said. "We could be dealing with embezzlement of funds, or it might involve the waiters or waitresses."

He stirred the tea in his glass, then looked back at Jill. "As an insider, you might be able to get some servers to talk."

"That would be our hope," I said.

"What kind of fee are we talking about?"

When I told him, he nodded.

"Sounds reasonable. Let me get with corporate and be sure we're all singing from the same hymnbook. We should be ready to start something in a day or so."

The prospects appeared so favorable that I blew the budget and ordered an exotic-looking dessert for the three of us. While we waited, Logan told us about being raised by his grandmother in the projects in Birmingham. She had done a heroic job of molding him into the successful young businessman who sat across from us.

When the dessert came, it was a monstrous concoction of cake and ice cream and various toppings. One serving would have done for the three of us. Or so I thought, though Jill and Logan demolished their portions rather thoroughly. After coffee and a final bit of friendly banter, we shook hands, I paid the check, Logan shouldered his golf bag for the trip to his room, and Jill and I headed back out to the lobby.

To our dismay, we found the scene there pure bedlam. Uniformed officers stood at every outside door, barring anyone from leaving the building. A police sergeant shouted orders. Desk clerks and bellmen scurried about in complete confusion. Clusters of guests, many wearing convention badges, chattered like seagulls on the beach beside our Florida condo, their faces twisted in bewilderment.

Jill stared. "What in the world is going on?"

"I don't know," I said. "It's obviously not a meeting of the Greg McKenzie Fan Club."

As I looked about, I recognized a few Metro detectives in plain clothes questioning people in the lobby. Happily, my old nemesis, Murder Squad Detective Mark Tremaine, was not among them. But after searching the crowd a few moments, I spotted Phil Adamson talking to a stocky young man in a black windbreaker I thought I remembered as an FBI agent. Oh, for the good old days when the feds only wore conservative blue suits. At any rate, obviously something major had taken place.

I steered Jill toward where Phil stood, his face pinched into its usual dour expression. Though not impressive to look at—tall, gaunt, with thinning brown hair and a beak of a nose that appeared slightly out of joint—Adamson was a sharp, intelligent cop. Assigned to Homicide, he and his colleagues investigated other violent crimes in addition to murders.

As he turned away from the FBI guy, I tapped him on the shoulder.

He looked around, raising both eyebrows. "What the hell are you doing here, McKenzie?"

I grinned. "Having lunch with the client you sent our way, Phil. Thanks for the recommendation. What's happening?"

He glanced toward Jill. "Hi, Miz McKenzie." After looking around to check nearby faces, he lowered his voice, which had a somber, gravelly quality. "Somebody just shot Dr. Elliott Bernstein. Very dead."

"The Fed chairman?" I recalled reading in the paper that he would be in town for a meeting at the local Federal Reserve Bank and to speak at the securities dealers convention.

"Right," Adamson said with a nod. "Looks like an execution."

2

It was after two o'clock by the time we reached the office. The drive hardly took twenty minutes, but there had been the inevitable delays while the police, the FBI and the Secret Service tried to put things at Opryworld into some sort of perspective. Thanks to the intervention of Detective Adamson, we were allowed through the hotel's guarded exit without excessive hassle. However, it didn't take an old-time investigator to deduce the reason for the dark looks I got from a few of the cops at the door. Too many in the ranks still viewed me as something of an enemy.

We had scanned the radio dial on the way to the office but learned little more than we already knew about the Opryworld affair. Dr. Elliott Bernstein, chairman of the Federal Reserve Board, whom some people called the second most powerful man in the country, had been killed by a gunshot while being escorted through the Governors' Lobby by a group of convention officials and his two Secret Service bodyguards. Both Metro Police and the FBI were on the scene, but no one in an official position had commented on who the killer might have been or what could be the motive. The media, however, had already plunged headfirst into what it does best, speculating wildly on the possibilities. In the wake of the World Trade Center tragedy, the Iraq war, and continuing problems with Al Qaida, they called it a likely terrorist act.

At any rate, all was calm at the office of McKenzie Investigations when we showed up at the strip center a few miles from our home in Hermitage. This suburb on the southeastern side of Nashville was named after Andrew Jackson's historic home. Being a native of St. Louis, I wasn't all that conversant with our seventh president until the Air Force sent me down here as a short-haired shavetail in the sixties. After meeting Jill, I was quickly enlightened on the Jacksonian references that abounded in the area. Old Hickory Boulevard, for instance, which is our office address, came from the general's nickname.

Although "boulevard" sounds fairly grand, our office was not. The space had been occupied until recently by a small beauty shop. The large window in front offered little in the way of privacy—not a good selling point for clients who preferred anonymity. We had discussed painting it with some kind of mural but couldn't agree on the scene. Jill wanted a seashore with palm trees. I opted for mountains with colorful hardwoods. The only privacy we could offer at present lay in the rear, namely a storage room and a small bath. Up front McKenzie Investigations, being an equal opportunity employer, provided identical his and hers desks, small but adequate. Client chairs, a file cabinet, a paper shredder that gobbled up no-longer-needed working papers, and a narrow table for the essentials—coffee maker, fax, copy machine/printer and small TV—occupied the rest of the space. Our lone computer sat on Jill's desk. As the only financial genius in the family, she served as treasurer.

I gathered the mail, mostly junk, from beneath the door slot and took it to my desk. Jill stashed her handbag in a drawer, then headed for the miscellany table.

"Let's see if the TV folks have learned anything new," she said.

I started tossing junk mail. "Or guessed at anything more deviously."

I had picked up an envelope that showed a possibility of interest when the door opened and a woman wearing a short brown skirt and a well-filled green sweater walked in. She appeared thirtyish at first glance, though I upped that estimate by a few years when I saw the crow's feet in the corners of large gray eyes. She had long reddish-brown hair and a shapely body that she maneuvered seductively as she crossed the room. I found her face attractive, even with a troubled cast to her eyes.

"Can we help you?" I asked.

"I hope so," she said, stopping halfway to my desk. She glanced across at Jill. "You're the McKenzies?"

I smiled. "Right on both counts." I motioned to one of the client chairs. "Won't you have a seat, Miss—?"

"Molly," she said. "Molly Saint."

I was glad it wasn't Saint Molly. She really didn't fit my vision of somebody ready for canonization. Apparently not my wife's, either. Jill quickly switched off the TV, strode over and leaned against the side of her desk as Molly took a seat across from me.

"I'm Jill McKenzie," she said. "This is my husband, Greg."

I thought she put a little more emphasis than necessary on the husband part, but I suppose it's a woman thing.

"How can we help you?" I asked.

"It's a problem with my husband," Molly said.

Jill gave her a sympathetic smile. "I'm sorry, Mrs. Saint, but we don't handle domestic relations cases. We can give you the names of some other agencies that do."

Molly Saint had placed her denim-clad handbag on the floor. Now she twisted her hands in her lap. "It's not what you're thinking," she said. "I'm not looking for somebody to snoop around and catch him in bed with another woman. I haven't decided about a divorce."

She had a voice that sounded somewhat argumentative. It made you want to hold up your hands and say *okay, I believe you*. I leaned my elbows on the desk. "Then what's the problem?"

"I want you to do what I guess you'd call a background investigation on Damon."

"How long have you been married?" Jill asked.

"About five years."

I shook my head. "Isn't it a bit late to be checking on his background now?"

She lowered her eyes. "Probably."

"Then what are you looking for?" I asked.

"I'm not sure."

I tried to keep my voice from mirroring the skepticism I felt. "So why check him out at all?"

She stopped twisting her hands and looked up. "I'm afraid of him."

Jill frowned. "Has he been beating you up?"

"No."

"Threatened you?"

"Not exactly."

"Have you been to the police about this?" I asked.

"They say there's no grounds for them to do anything, so they won't. But I know he's capable of violent things. I don't think he realized I was watching, but a couple of months ago I saw him take a large knife—like a machete—and go after a neighborhood dog that kept barking at him."

"That's horrible," Jill said, cringing. "Did he hurt the dog?"

"No. Thank God the dog got away." Seeing Jill's sympathetic reaction, Molly turned to her. "I'm really scared. If I tell him I'm leaving, he'll do something terrible to me. I know he will."

"Then don't tell him," I said. "Just take off. Leave a note if you want to."

"He'd come after me," she said, shaking her head. "I can't quit my job. I've worked too hard to get where I am."

"Where do you work?" Jill asked.

"Maxxim Motor Freight Lines. I'm taking a few days off. My nerves are shot."

She didn't look all that stressed out to me. I also couldn't picture her in the cab of an eighteen-wheeler but couldn't resist asking. "Do you drive a truck?"

That brought a frown I took as irritation. "No. I'm an administrative assistant. I work directly under Mr. Crenshaw, the owner."

I had heard of Grant Crenshaw. He was a wheeler and dealer around Nashville, owning several large office buildings among other investments. He had started out with the truck line and had a reputation as a hard-driving businessman, the quintessential laissez-faire entrepreneur.

"Has your husband done anything else that concerns you?" Jill asked.

"I just feel it in my bones," she said. "It's the way he looks at me. Things he doesn't say. Damon was in Vietnam. One of the drivers at work told me about some guys who fought over there. He said they did some real nasty things when they came back."

I'd about had enough of Miss Molly and her goofy generalizations. "That was thirty years ago," I said. "Those guys are either in prison or mental hospitals or living on the streets. Most of the guys who fought in Vietnam are no different from the rest of us. I doubt you have anything to worry about. If your husband should start stalking you or making threats, you can go to court and get a restraining order."

Jill grimaced. "Come on, Greg. You know how that works. Restraining orders don't restrain men determined to do bodily harm. Why don't we find out a little more before we make any judgments?"

My wife can be so damned rational at times.

"Tell us about Damon, how you met him?" Jill asked. She wheeled the chair out from behind her desk and sat facing Molly.

The young woman rubbed her cheek with one hand and looked around. "You got a water fountain? My mouth's awful dry."

"How about coffee?" I asked. We were coffee drinkers, first and foremost.

"Just water'll be fine."

We didn't have a water fountain, but we had a supply of soft drinks in a small refrigerator in the storeroom. "We've got Cokes, Sprite, that sort of thing," I said.

"A Coke would be nice," she said.

I headed to the back room as Jill rephrased her last question. "How did you meet Damon?"

"It was around five years ago," she said. With the door open, I could easily hear her reply. "I had just broken up with this guy I'd been with for quite a while. I was at this bar having a few drinks one night and somebody suddenly started talking beside me. He was a very ordinary-looking guy, you know. I hadn't paid any attention to him before that. Anyway, when he spoke he had this deep voice like a radio announcer. Only he talked real soft like and polite."

She accepted the Coke can and a plastic cup with a silently mouthed thanks.

"So he wasn't the handsome prince?" Jill said with a grin.

"Hardly. But there was something attractive about him. He was around your height, lots of muscles, long black hair. I never went for guys with long hair before that. I guess it was the eyes that really got to me, though. They're dark as night, and when he looked at me, I felt like he was seeing right down into my soul. Whatever he saw, he must have liked. He asked me out the next day."

"Was it a very long courtship?" Jill asked.

"Ha!" She took a swallow of Coke. "I went out with him two or three times and suddenly he wanted to marry me. Like I said, I was on the rebound. He seemed nice enough. What the hell, I thought. Why not?"

I figured there was more to it than that. Most likely some shenanigans in the bedroom she didn't care to go into.

"So you married him," Jill said. "How much did you know about him at that time?"

"Not enough, obviously."

"How about some specifics," I said.

She sipped on the Coke, then twisted the cup in her hands. "Well, he said he was raised in an orphanage and had no family."

"Where was he raised?" I asked.

"Chicago."

A big city. It could be a little difficult to check out but was no big deal. "What did he tell you about his military service?"

"Said he served in Vietnam. He retired from the Army later and lived mostly on his pension."

"How much pension does he get?"

"He never said. It goes directly to his bank account, which is separate from mine."

She was certainly on target when she said her knowledge of her husband was pretty meager.

"You say he lives mostly on his pension. What else does he do?" I asked.

"He works for Heritage Car Rentals. Ferries cars back and forth between local and out-of-town offices. They let him work as much or as little as he wants to."

"Is he working today?" Jill asked.

She nodded as she finished her Coke. "I called the office. He left for Chattanooga this morning. That's why I came over here now."

Jill turned to me. "What do you think, Greg?"

I spread my hands and looked at Molly. "Nothing you've told us raises any major alarms. Apparently he didn't harm the dog you mentioned. He was probably just chasing it off. I still don't see any reason to panic. And I have no idea what you want us to look for."

Molly clasped her hands again, stared down at them, then back up at me. "I guess I'd just like to know more about him. You know, has he been in any trouble? Has he hurt anybody? I want to know if my fears are real or just imagination."

Before I could reply, Jill jumped in. "Let us talk it over tonight, Mrs. Saint. We'll give you our decision in the morning."

That was not the reply I had intended to give. I sometimes wondered about this monster I had created when I let Jill talk me into her being a detective and my partner in crime. She had even bought a small revolver that would fit in her handbag and took firing lessons, despite having expressed great reservations over the necessity of my carrying a gun while on active duty. She did really well on the range, though with that little .38 the targets weren't too far away. My choice of weapon was a 9mm

Beretta a bit smaller than the one I was issued in the Air Force. We both had permits to carry concealed weapons but, like most private investigators, saw no need to carry them routinely.

At any rate, I heard Molly exhale sharply as I sat there looking flustered.

"Don't call me," she said. "I seldom know where he's gonna be. I'll call you."

3

THE PHONE RANG as Jill accompanied Molly Saint to the door. Jesse Logan greeted me with word that he needed a little more embellishment on my ideas regarding how to pursue the King Cole's investigation. I had been talking off the top of my head during lunch and told him quite frankly what I had in mind only amounted to bare bones at the moment. I would need more time to flesh out the plan. However, I did some quick improvisation and came up with enough meat to hopefully satisfy his bosses.

"I guess you got caught in the same dragnet I did after lunch," he said when we finished our business.

"Right. Did you get interrogated by the cops?"

"Did I," he said, a note of irritation in his voice. "After I finally convinced them I was a guest in the hotel and had just eaten lunch in the Lakeside restaurant, they let me go. I had no idea what was going on until after I got to my room and turned on the TV."

"We've been too busy to check out the tube," I said. "What's the latest?"

"According to the last I heard on CNN, I'd say there was a little friction between the FBI and your local police. An FBI spokesman said it appears to be the work of a professional assassin. He said it could be a conspiracy that relates to Bernstein's position with the Fed. The Nashville police chief leans to the theory that it might have been somebody local with a grudge against the chairman."

"They have any evidence of that?"

"Seems the Fed office in Washington received a threatening letter from Nashville several months ago. It was anonymous."

"Looks like they have their work cut out for them."

"Yeah," Logan said. "The cops apparently think the murder was committed by a black male who's a present or former employee of the hotel."

"So that's why you got the treatment," I said. "I'm sorry about that. I hope you won't hold it against us."

"Hey," he said, "you guys had nothing to do with it. In fact, I understand you've had your own troubles with the local gendarmes."

"Where did you hear that?"

"Detective Adamson. He said it was all a big misunderstanding, that I shouldn't believe anything I might hear about it."

"Phil's a good guy. By the way, did CNN say what brought on the black employee theory?"

"Something about a black guy in a black hat and trench coat seen heading through an employee exit."

When I got off the phone, I told Jill what Logan had said about the Bernstein murder and his request for more details on our investigation. She quickly let me know she had more interest in Logan's problems than those of the police and the FBI. I did, too, of course, but I couldn't ignore the lure of a high-profile murder case.

"What kind of initial retainer do you think we'll get from Leisure Foods?" she asked.

I scratched my chin, entertaining thoughts about what this case might lead to in the future. "Enough to take care of the office for a few months, I'd think."

The rent wasn't all that much, but the overhead included lights and water and telephone. Fortunately, our interest in the agency didn't center primarily on the money. It might be more properly called a rehabilitation project. I equated the term "retiree" with being put out to pasture, and I had no desire to lie around and eat grass. But the Air Force had declined to promote me to full colonel and cited regulations that insisted I had overstayed my welcome in the service. After re-locating to Jill's hometown, I quickly found I had enjoyed all the leisure I could stand and took a job as an investigator for the DA. Then came the big flap over my comments in the newspaper about Detective Tremaine. The DA insisted I retire again. After I took on the task of solving the murder of a friend's son in Florida last fall, Jill was nearly ecstatic. She said I acted like a new man. Not merely new, but someone with a purpose and, even more gratifying to her, a man with a pleasant disposition—

something I had apparently lacked during my latest round of forced inaction. Since she had been a major factor in solving the Florida slaying, she proposed that we start our own detective agency, picking and choosing the cases we wanted to pursue.

"Let's talk about Molly Saint," I said.

I sat behind my desk, arms folded, head cocked at just the right angle, looking very judgmental and not at all compromising.

Grinning, Jill walked over and put an arm around my shoulder. "I had thought we would save that for pillow talk."

I looked askance. "I'm shocked, babe. You would stoop to using womanly wiles to sway a business decision?"

Spinning my chair around, she plopped into my lap and looked up with those big brown eyes that made you feel in danger of falling in and drowning. "Unconscionable," I murmured, then laid a big kiss on her.

Pulling away, I shifted my head and looked toward the front window. "What's that boy staring at?"

Jill jumped off my lap and turned toward the window, straightening her skirt. She frowned. "What boy?"

"Just kidding," I said with a chuckle. "You'll have to admit it would've made a pretty steamy scene if a potential client had walked in."

She punched me in the ribs. "You dog. I'd have told them I was just your secretary asking for a raise."

"Well, you certainly got a rise out of me."

She shook her head and returned to her desk. "I think we should take Molly Saint as a client."

"I'm not sure her carpet goes wall-to-wall," I said.

"Why?"

"That bit about feeling it in her bones. Things he doesn't say. Unfounded inferences because he was a Vietnam vet. Hell, she married him on a lark. What did she expect?"

"I'm sure she didn't expect to be frightened out of her wits. The look in her eyes was fear, Greg. Fear with a capital F."

"I have some reservations about that."

"There's another thing that concerns me." She continued right on as though I hadn't spoken. "There's something vaguely familiar about Molly. I'm sure we've never met before, but it's...well, I have this eerie feeling about her."

I had often spoken of hunches I'd had on cases, about going with my intuition. I figured that's what she was driving at.

"What about King Cole's?" I asked. "We'll probably have our hands full with that."

"Logan said they wouldn't be ready for a day or so. It shouldn't take long to check out Mr. Damon Saint. If something is really wrong, you don't want to be responsible for what might happen to that young woman, do you?"

I let out a deep breath that must have sounded like what it was, a sigh of capitulation.

"Okay," I said. "We'll take the case. But if there's any inkling that she's gone off the deep end or lied about any of this, we'll cut her off in a flash. I don't care if she's Saint Molly or Saint Mary. And we'll demand a healthy advance against our fee."

4

MOLLY SAINT CALLED FROM A PAY PHONE the next morning at nine, just after we arrived at the office. Jill took the call and gave her the good news—from her point of view. Molly agreed to come by at ten and provide all the information she could on her husband, including his Social Security number and a photograph.

She arrived in skin-tight jeans and a brown denim shirt open so low I found myself searching for a glimpse of her navel. Pulling a chair in between the two desks, she sat down, reached into her bag and slipped out a color photo. I took it from her and laid it on the corner of my desk. Jill scooted her chair over and joined me in studying the picture.

"Must be your wedding," Jill said.

Molly nodded.

The photo showed her wearing a dark green suit and a

broad smile, a corsage of red carnations pinned to her shoulder. The man at her side, whose hand she clutched, wore a gray pinstripe suit, no flowers. However, he didn't impress me as being the pinstripe type. He was stocky, a little taller than Molly, almost black hair down to his shoulders and intense black eyes that mirrored no happiness over the occasion. I wondered if he'd had second thoughts about the quick proposal.

"Don't you have a more recent photo of Damon by himself?" I asked.

She shook her head. "He doesn't like pictures. Won't have a camera in the house. I don't know if it's something he picked up in Vietnam or where, but he says he's one of those people who believe taking your picture steals a part of your soul."

I'd heard that about some primitive tribes, but Damon Saint did not impress me as being an aboriginal.

"Does he still wear his hair long?" I asked.

"No," she said. "It's about like yours."

I took that to mean he looked like an average guy, with maybe a small balding spot in back. While I doubted the term "average" applied to me particularly well overall, my hair and a few other features probably fell into that category.

"How old is Damon?" Jill asked.

"Mid-fifties."

"And you're around forty?"

She grinned. "Good guess."

I pushed the photo aside and looked back at her. "How long has he worked for Heritage Car Rentals?"

"I think maybe a year or so before we met. I know he mentioned living in an apartment not far from the Heritage office."

"Where do you live now?"

She gave an address in Antioch, a suburb on the south side of town that bordered Priest Lake, a large man-made body of water backed up by J. Percy Priest Dam.

"It's a little rental house," she said. "Damon moved in a year before we got married."

"Do you live near the lake?" I asked.

"Within a few blocks."

"Does he like to fish, maybe? Hunt?"

"No."

"What does he do in his spare time?"

"He runs a lot."

Jill glanced back at the photo. "You mean he's a jogger?"

"A runner. He doesn't do marathons, but he runs just about every day."

"Any hobbies?" I asked.

"Well, he makes jewelry."

I straightened up in surprise. "Jewelry?"

"Yeah," Molly said. "Kinda wild, isn't it? He has this workshop in the basement. He's given me a few pieces." She held out her right hand. "He made this little diamond ring. I also have a ruby necklace and a few other pieces."

I got up and moved around to the front of the desk for a closer look. "Where did he learn to do that?"

She shrugged. "I have no clue."

"What does he do with the stuff he makes?" I asked.

"Sometimes he goes to flea markets."

Jill was studying the ring. "That's very nice. He must have a lot of small tools in his workshop."

"I wouldn't know," she said. "I've never been down there."

I gave her a skeptical look. "In five years, you've never seen his workshop?"

"He says it's very tedious work. He doesn't want anybody interfering with his concentration."

"I can't believe you haven't sneaked a peek when he wasn't at home."

"He keeps the door locked. Can't blame him there. If somebody knew what he had, they could come in and steal him blind."

"Mrs. Saint, if a thief wanted in, he would jimmy the lock."

"Well, he'd be sorry if he did," she said. "Damon says the door's booby trapped. I don't know what it would do, but he'd sure as hell know if anyone tried to steal some of his jewelry."

"What about friends?" I asked, taking a different tack. "Does he have any close friends at work, or elsewhere?"

"Not really." She hesitated, reconsidering. "Well, maybe."

"What do you mean?"

"He has some old Vietnam buddies. I don't know any names. But once in a while he takes off to go help one. Says it's sort of like being an AA member. If one has a problem, he calls for help. The others rally to his side."

"They must really be a tight-knit bunch," Jill said.

I knew a bit about that. I had put in some time in Vietnam. But infantry types who had to live together and survive together were more likely to form bonds that lasted long beyond the war.

I reminded Molly of her comments yesterday about being afraid of her husband because of the way he looked at her, things he didn't say. "What exactly did you mean by that?"

She gave a twist to her mouth and stammered a bit. "Well, I guess…for one thing…we don't go out a lot. To a restaurant once in a great while, or a Predators game. Damon loves hockey. I've got this girl friend at work I go out with more than I do Damon. She and I go shopping a lot or to a movie. He'd rather watch movies at home."

"So what are you saying? Did he refuse to take you somewhere?"

"I'd been bugging him for weeks to go to a concert. I complained that if he could take off at a moment's notice to spend a week helping an old buddy, he should be able to spend one night with me at the Gaylord Center."

An arena that housed the NHL Nashville Predators, the Gaylord Center also catered to rock concerts, country music extravaganzas, you name it. Since she still hadn't given me the answer I was looking for, I asked, "So what happened?"

"When I brought it up again about a week ago, he glared at me with those cold black eyes and said, 'Get your damned friend Peggy to go with you. If you don't get off my ass–' He never finished it, but I knew what he meant. I would be eternally sorry."

"But he hasn't done anything to you," I said.

"Not physically…yet. He's been in a dark mood the last few months, though. I'm sure it's only a matter of time. Meanwhile, he just does whatever he pleases and to hell with me. I've had it. I'd leave him today if I wasn't so damned scared."

While I was digesting that, Jill got down to business. "What about his Social Security number, Molly?"

She pulled a small piece of paper out of her handbag. "I had to search all over the place to find it."

"Don't you keep copies of your tax returns?" I asked.

"I have mine, of course," she said. "We file separate. Damon said it would be better that way."

I should have known.

"Is he working at Heritage today?" I asked.

She nodded. "He had to go to Crossville. He shouldn't be back until after lunch."

I took the slip with the Social Security number and the wedding photo and put them in a folder I had prepared for the case file. I gave Jill a prompting glance.

She turned to Molly. "Did you bring the money for the fee advance?"

Molly pulled a checkbook out of her bag, tore off a check and handed it over. "Eight hundred dollars."

"That should cover everything," Jill said. "If there's any left over after we figure our time and expenses, we'll return it to you."

Molly looked up. "I can give you more if necessary."

"This is fine for now," Jill said. "We'll be in touch with you when we have something."

Molly shook her head. "I'll call you. Say in a couple of days?"

"That will be fine."

"What if there's an emergency? Do you have a cell phone?"

Jill wrote the number on the back of a business card. "We keep it on when we're away from the office. But your best bet is to call us here or at home."

Molly took the card and started toward the door, then stopped and looked back. "Please be careful how you handle this. Don't say any more than you have to to anybody. I just pray that Damon doesn't get wind of what I've done."

5

I SAT AT MY DESK WITH A YELLOW PAD finishing my notes on the Molly Saint interview. Picking up my coffee mug, I stared into it. Empty.

"Coming up, dear," Jill said from across the office. She brought the pot over, poured the steaming brew and glanced down at my almost illegible scrawling. "It would make things a lot easier if you would do that on the computer."

I darted her a pained look. "Give me a little time, babe. I still think better with a pen in hand. I'll transfer it to the computer."

She did the old eye roll maneuver, as though following the path of a rainbow, her favorite way of expressing irritation at some of my questionable antics. "Okay, boss," she said. "Where do we start with this?"

Boss was the nickname OSI agents used in referring to their special agent in charge. Jill had started using it—tongue-in-cheek, I hasten to add—since the opening of McKenzie Investigations. The only other person who still referred to me that way was Ted Kennerly, OSI special agent in charge at Arnold Air Force Base seventy miles south of Nashville. He had served under me several years ago fresh out of the Special Investigations Academy. Present for the not-so-grand opening of our Old Hickory Boulevard office, Ted had insisted that we call him when we had problems he could help with.

"I think we'd better ask Ted to check with the Army on Mr. Saint," I said. "I'll make a few other inquiries, then we can head over to Heritage Car Rentals and see what they know."

I caught Ted in his office and asked him if he would run down the facts on Damon Saint's military service.

"No problem," he said. "How's the PI business? We've been picking up vibrations all the way down here over that Bernstein shooting. You know anything about it?"

I told him our experience during and after lunch at the hotel.

He chuckled. "Glad we're just involved with simple things like terrorists and druggies. I'll check out your man Saint and get back to you as soon as I have something."

Consulting my list that showed which of the first three digits in Social Security numbers were assigned to each state, I found Damon Saint had received his card while living in Indiana. He claimed to have been raised in Chicago, which was where a lot of people in northern Indiana worked.

Finances can tell a lot about a person. A bit of knowledge about Damon Saint's finances would give me a better insight into him, how he lived, where he traveled, what he was involved in. Molly had provided precious little help. Clearly, he did not want her to know anything regarding his financial situation. We had signed with a few on-line companies that could provide a world of information on subjects under investigation, but I decided to try an intriguing source I had learned of from a friend several weeks back.

David Wolfson had come to my aid a year and a half ago while I was working to free Jill from a group that had taken her hostage. The co-owner of a local market research firm, David was a computer geek. Back in his college days, he had been part of a hacker group and later worked for the National Security Agency. Recently he'd told me about a young Hispanic he had met through a former buddy in the network. Julio de Leon specialized in "researching" the U.S. financial system. According to David, if there was anything to be found about an individual's accounts—checking, savings, brokerage, credit cards, you name it—Julio could find it.

I looked up his number and got Julio on the phone. I told him who I was and that David Wolfson had recommended him.

"Greg McKenzie, you say?"

"That's right. I'm a private investigator."

"Hold a sec." Julio was back a few moments later. "You recently opened a business account for McKenzie Investigations. Co-signer Jill McKenzie."

I shook my head. "Okay. I'm impressed."

"Good," he said. "David told me I should be hearing from you. What took you so long?"

"Up to now I hadn't found a need for your services."

"Obviously that's changed."

"It has, and I'd be *mucho* obliged if you could help."

"Aha, now you're speaking my language."

"I guess I was," I said, though not intentionally. After studying Spanish in high school and college, *mucho* just popped up on occasion. "David told me you came up from Mexico with your parents. You speak English like a native."

"*Sí*. Eef you prefer I speak like the Espanish, I can do that."

"Never mind," I said. "I need to see what you can find on a guy named Damon Saint."

"He one of those who came marching in?"

I had a joker on my hands. "Probably. He was in the Army."

"What else can you tell me about him?"

"How about a Social Security number?"

"Couldn't do better."

I read off the number.

"Are you looking for anything special?" he asked.

"No, nothing special. Just whatever you can dig up. He's pretty much a blank at this point."

"If he has any accounts, I'll find them. Guar-on-teed. You in a hurry?"

"I'd like something by tomorrow, if possible."

"How about this afternoon?"

"Great. What's it going to cost me?"

He laughed. "A new client, first inquiry...I just might do this one gratis."

When I repeated what Julio had said, Jill frowned. "We're not going to get in any trouble, are we?"

I gave a little shrug. "Not unless the feds have a wiretap on us."

IT WAS AROUND ELEVEN when I turned my Jeep Grand Cherokee into the paved lot at the Heritage Car Rentals office on Murfreesboro Road, not far from Nashville International Airport. This part of the city was not the most scenic. A conglomeration of nondescript small businesses dotted with fast food outlets appeared thrown together like a pickup basketball team. The day was warm, the temperature in the upper sixties. I parked between a vintage red Corvette with the top down and a big black pickup. The place resembled a small auto dealership, with cars, vans and SUV's lined up on the tarmac. Red, white and blue balloons bobbed about in the morning breeze.

Jill and I entered the office, which had a glassed-in front that made it look like a small auto showroom. Posters mounted around the windows promoted special weekend rates and vacation deals—airfare, hotel room, car, all in one neat package. A long counter with several computer stations occupied one side of the room. Offices lined the other, the first one labeled MANAGER.

"What kind of car can we fix you up with?" asked a tall, muscular black man behind the counter. He had a Clark Gable mustache and a Rhett Butler grin.

"No car, thanks," I said. "Is the manager in?"

"That's his little red toy you parked beside. Name's Art Finley. He's in his office." The man pointed to the door beyond the counter. "He just got off the phone. You can knock and go on in."

I didn't like the idea of barging in without an invitation, so I walked over to the door, knocked and waited.

"Come in," someone yelled from beyond the door.

Jill and I entered to find a short, stocky man seated behind a gray metal desk. It occupied one side of a modest-sized office decorated with plaques and certificates honoring the agency for outstanding performance in areas such as sales and maintenance. I noticed the dates on them were all pre-millennium. Arthur Finley, whose name was confirmed by the walnut plaque on the desk, evidently doted on past glory.

"What can I do for you folks?" Finley asked, getting up from his desk. The wide grin looked almost cherubic on a round face topped by a horseshoe-shaped fringe of white. I judged him to be around sixty, more than five years my junior.

I handed him my card, which said "McKenzie Investigations, Background Checks, Civil and Criminal Investigations, Greg & Jill McKenzie, More than 30 Years Law Enforcement Experience." The experience, of course, was all mine.

Finley motioned us to a couple of chairs.

"We'd like to ask you a few questions about one of your employees," I said. My smile was meant to be disarming. "He's not suspected of any wrongdoing. We're just looking into his background for a client."

Finley frowned. "Which employee?"

"Damon Saint."

"I guess you know he's just part-time. He apply for a full-time job?"

"No," I said. "This isn't a pre-employment check. How long has he worked for you?"

He sat back in his chair, looking thoughtful. "Seven years. Maybe eight. Was a couple of years after I sold my little used car lot and came with Heritage. Probably should have stayed where I was. Don't mind saying I was one helluva car salesman."

Jill grinned. "I'll bet you sold all the ladies."

"I did that, all right. Never met a lady I didn't like." He chuckled. "Probably why the wife left me."

"Did Damon tell you about his military service?" I asked.

"Yeah. He's retired Army. That's one reason I took him on. I try to give veterans a preference in hiring. My kid brother was killed in Vietnam."

"Sorry to hear that," I said. "Did Damon mention that he had served over there?"

"Yeah. I told him about my brother, Donnie. Donnie died back in the early sixties. He was a Green Beret. Damon said he knew some Special Forces guys in Vietnam. He must've had it pretty rough. He doesn't want to talk about it. I guess a lot of them feel that way."

I nodded. "I was in Nam for a while. In the Air Force. Incidentally, I understand Damon has his military pension deposited directly to his bank account. Is that the way you pay him?"

Finley shook his head. "No way. Damon likes to feel the long green. I sorta like the feel of it myself. There's a bank across the road. That's where he heads as soon as he gets his check."

"Do you know his wife Molly, Mr. Finley?" Jill asked.

"Oh, yeah. I've met her." He did a little dance with his

shoulders. "Sexy looking girl. Wouldn't say I really know her, but we've met. A real odd couple, if you ask me."

"In what way?"

"I don't know how they ever got together. He doesn't strike me as being her type."

Jill cocked an eyebrow. "What type is that?"

Finley picked up a small glass paperweight and rolled it around in his hand. "Have you met her?"

"Yes," Jill said.

"Wouldn't you say she looks like the party type? Well, I can't see old Damon partying, except maybe with a beer at the corner tavern."

"He like to hoist one with the guys?" I asked.

"Occasionally. Some of 'em drop by a little joint down Murfreesboro Road nearly every afternoon. Damon goes once in a while."

"These are people who ferry cars like Damon?"

"Yeah."

"Retirees like Damon?"

"Mostly."

"Is Damon working today?"

Finley nodded and set his glass toy on a stack of papers. "That's his big black Dodge Ram diesel parked out front. He's by himself today. Sometimes two or three of them travel in a convoy. They ride together on the way back if they're only bringing one car."

"Does he get along pretty well with the other guys?" I asked.

"The only complaint I've heard is he doesn't talk much. Just sits there like a cigar store Indian."

"The others must be big talkers."

"Some of them will drive you up the wall."

"Does Damon talk to you?" I asked.

"He answers questions. I figure maybe it has something to do with too much time in combat. Probably got a lot of stuff he's holding inside. You know, stuff he doesn't want to talk about."

Before leaving, I asked Finley to keep our conversation confidential. We had given no hint that Molly had any connection with our investigation, but if her husband became aware of our inquiries, he might correctly assume she had something to do with it.

I knew from the interview with Molly that Damon didn't talk a lot. But I wasn't so sure of Art Finley's diagnosis about the reason for it. I was getting the picture of a loner who preferred to play everything close to the vest. It seemed the more we learned about him, the greater the enigma Damon Saint was turning into. I was anxious to find out what Julio de Leon and Ted Kennerly had learned about him.

6

Jill and I drove a little farther out Murfreesboro Road past the Dell Computer complex and stopped for lunch at a Subway restaurant. Ever since some character had come on TV with the story that he had lost a hundred or so pounds on a diet of Subway sandwiches, my wife had pushed me toward half a foot of meat and veggies on a wheat bun as one way to maintain my girlish figure. It seems I have a problem with a tendency to overeat when the pressure gets too great. Since my life had remained on a pretty steady course in recent months, however, my weight was currently one of the least of my worries.

We arrived back at the office about the same time as a white panel truck with "Computers 'n Stuff" painted on the side.

"Must be the new printer," Jill said. The old one printed only in black. We needed one that would turn out color photographs for use as evidence.

I unlocked the office door as the driver, a muscular black man, stepped out of the truck and went to the back, where he slid out a large box faced with the image of an expensive-looking printer. Being the Scot that I am, I wasn't sure we needed to spend that kind of money, but office equipment was Jill's department. She walked in ahead of the man and showed him where to put the carton.

"Want me to open it for you?" he asked.

He had a solemn look and seemed a bit surly. Since he was bald it couldn't have been a bad hair day. "Never mind," I said. "I can take care of it."

He pulled a sheaf of papers from his shirt pocket and pointed to a line with an X. "Need you to sign here."

I turned to Jill. "Is this what you ordered, babe?"

She checked the box and nodded. "It should make you look like a pro."

"I thought I was a pro."

"Just sign the receipt, Greg."

I signed and handed it back. "Thanks, Larry," I said, noting the name badge pinned to his shirt.

He nodded, maintaining that dour look, and gave me a copy of the receipt. I watched as he headed for the door, noticing an odd gait that might have come from an old leg injury. I still find myself doing tricks like that, observing anything that appears out of the ordinary. It's something that sticks with you long after the need is past. Turning back to the box, I took out my pocketknife and tackled the job of printer setup. While I tugged the new toy away from its packing, the phone rang.

"It's for you, pro," Jill said.

"I checked your man out thoroughly," said a businesslike Julio de Leon.

"What did you find?" I asked.

"What I didn't find might be more apropos. Damon Saint has no current checking accounts, no savings accounts, no bank accounts, *nada*. Furthermore, he has no credit or debit cards and no accounts with a stockbroker."

Maybe David Wolfson had overrated young Julio, I thought. Apparently he didn't have all the financial programs or passwords or whatever wizardry it took to get into the right files.

"In other words, you struck out," I said.

Julio's voice had a wounded sound. "I hope that doesn't imply what I think it does, Mr. McKenzie, that I failed to find something that exists out there in financial cyberspace. I can assure you nothing currently exists for the name and Social Security number you gave me."

"Sorry," I said. "I didn't mean to question your competence. It's just hard to believe he has no accounts. His wife said his military pension payments were made directly to his bank."

"Then she lied. Now if you're interested in his past activity, that's a different matter."

"What does that mean?"

"From the middle eighties to the middle nineties, Mr. Saint had multiple accounts in Indianapolis, Indiana."

The Social Security number from Indiana. Of course. It fit.

"What kind of accounts?" I asked.

"Both personal and business. He also had credit cards."

"What business?"

"Pro-Kleen Carpet Care." He spelled it out for me.

"Sounds like a franchise deal," I said.

"Probably."

"The accounts were closed in the mid-nineties?"

"The personal accounts were. The business account was transferred to another name."

"Meaning it was sold," I said.

"That would be my guess."

"Did you learn anything else about Damon Saint?"

"I checked the Indianapolis city directory for that period and found Mr. Saint had a house in the suburbs. So I took a look at the property records for the county. The house was sold a few months after Pro-Kleen Carpet Care apparently got its new owner. If Saint came to Nashville from there, I'd say he arrived with a pocketful of cash."

The time frame would have corresponded pretty well with Art Finley's recollection of when Saint had begun working with Heritage Car Rentals. But why had Damon lied to Molly about his Army pension going directly to his bank account? According to Julio, Damon had no bank account at all. What had happened to all the money he had brought with him from Indianapolis?

Jill and I were bouncing around these questions late that afternoon when Ted Kennerly called.

"Didn't your man Saint claim to have retired from the Army?" he asked.

"That's what he told his wife," I said.

"Well, ex-Sergeant Saint was being a bit untruthful. He

was discharged around the time the Vietnam War ended."

"So there was no retirement."

"None. He was given an honorable discharge and transportation back home to Indiana."

"That figures," I said. "What was his military assignment?"

"The Fifth Special Forces Group in Vietnam."

When I told Jill what I had learned about Damon, she shook her head. "Well, we know a little more about Mr. Saint," she said. "We know he's an accomplished liar. I'll bet he wasn't an orphan raised in Chicago, either."

"Quite likely. I think it might be worth our time to make a little junket to Indianapolis," I said. "Maybe somebody up there can tell us why he sold his house and his business and left Indiana."

7

WE LEFT EARLY THE NEXT MORNING for the flight to Indianapolis aboard Jill's Cessna. When I met her back in the sixties, she was a student in the aviation program at Middle Tennessee State College (now University), located in the next county to the south of Nashville. We married after her graduation, and her dad, a wealthy Nashville insurance man, gave her a Piper Cherokee so she could fly home whenever it suited her. A savvy businesswoman as well as an excellent pilot, Jill ran her own charter service for a time during my Air Force career. She still had a Cessna 172 that she kept at Cornelia Fort Air Park, not far from our home in Hermitage.

We took off into a cloudless blue sky and headed north, flying through air so smooth the plane could have been sliding along a greased track. I found that almost enough to make the flight a pleasure. Almost. But the fact remained, though I'd had to do a lot of flying during my years in the Air Force, I never enjoyed it. I equated being strapped into an airplane seat with being chained to an Inquisition-era torture device.

I brought the morning paper along in hopes of deluding myself into believing I had simply embarked upon a pleasant soiree among the heavens. I didn't fool my irrational mind, but I did get to bring myself up to date on the Bernstein affair. According to mostly unnamed sources, the FBI had concentrated on looking for the .22 rifle used in the slaying, plus questioning airline personnel regarding passengers departing Nashville International Airport on Monday afternoon. They had blown up stills from surveillance camera tapes, but the suspect's floppy hat, pulled down to hide his face, ruled out the chance of a positive identification.

As for Metro, the cops busied themselves interviewing Opryworld employees, hoping to find someone who had seen or heard something that might provide a clue to the murderer. They also sought anyone who likely harbored a grudge against the banking system.

Unfortunately, there was more airspace ahead than newspaper in my lap, but I managed to survive through the landing. For the sake of marital bliss, I skipped the kissing-of-the-ground ceremony at Indianapolis International Airport. After Jill shut down the engine on the private aircraft ramp, we headed for the fixed base operator's counter, where she took care of parking and servicing details and I checked the phone book for Pro-Kleen Carpet Care. The woman who answered informed me that the owner, Perry Vanatta, had left for a job. He could be reached on his cell phone, however.

When I contacted him, he agreed to meet us for lunch—I generously offered to buy—after finishing the current job, which involved cleaning carpets at a residence on the south side of the city. We met around 11:30 outside a small meat-and-three restaurant he had recommended, located in a large white frame house. Vanatta was tall and thin with close-cropped brown hair. He wore blue jeans and a gray knit shirt. His eyes seemed to blink almost constantly with a nervous tic.

After introductions, we strolled inside and were ushered to a small square table covered with a red and white checkered cloth. The waitress suggested the meat loaf, to which we obligingly agreed. After she left for the kitchen, I looked across at Vanatta.

"Thanks for agreeing to talk with us. Sounds like you're a busy man. How's the carpet cleaning business?"

"It just goes on and on. People keep getting them dirty and we keep cleaning up. Literally and figuratively. Boom or bust, not much changes."

"Must be nice," I said. "You told me on the phone that you knew Damon Saint. I take it you're the guy who bought the business from him?"

Folding his long, slender hands, he propped his sharp chin on them and blinked several times. "Actually, I didn't buy it. He gave it to me."

I gave him a skeptical look. "You're kidding."

Vanatta shook his head. "I had worked for him for about five years. When my dad died just after I graduated from high school, I was forced to forego college to support my mom and myself."

"That when you started with Damon?"

"Yeah. He only had one truck back then. But after I got pretty good at cleaning carpets, he bought another truck for me to use."

"Business was booming."

"Right. We were making a pretty decent living off it when all of a sudden he took off. No warning. No good-bye. Nothing."

I stared at him. "He disappeared?"

"Yeah. I came to work one Monday morning and the place looked abandoned. He just had a little hole-in-the-wall office. The business records were still there, but all of Damon's personal stuff was gone. Including his laptop computer, which he used to keep financial records and stuff like that."

"How long ago was this?"

"Around seven years ago."

"Did you ever hear from him?"

Vanatta paused, then nodded. "A few days later I got a letter."

"From where?"

"Louisville. He said he had agreed to take on a clandestine mission for the government."

This was getting a bit ridiculous. "Did you buy that?"

Vanatta shrugged. "Damon was always a big bull-shitter, if you'll pardon the expression. But the rest of the letter left me wondering. It said he was giving me the business—Pro-Kleen Carpet Care. He enclosed a signed, legal-looking statement of sale form that said he had sold everything to me, including the two trucks. The checking account was practically empty, but the bank signed what was left over to me."

"Did he ever call?"

"No. But something else was in the envelope. He enclosed a power of attorney giving me authorization to sell his house. Said he would contact me later about where to send the proceeds."

"He must have really trusted you," I said.

He blinked his eyes and nodded. "Yeah. He knew I had always played square with him."

The waitress brought our meat loaf with green beans, carrots and corn, and Vanatta related the rest of the story between bites. A couple of months later, he said, he received another letter from Saint. This one had an Atlanta postmark. Damon instructed him to send the money from the house sale to a box number in Atlanta. Vanatta had turned the house over to a Realtor, and when it sold fairly quickly, he forwarded the check as instructed.

"Did you hear anything else after that?" I asked.

"Nothing. He was sometimes a bit of a weird character, but I never expected anything like this. It worked out fine for me, though. I've expanded the business and run three trucks now."

"Did you know about Damon's service in Vietnam?"

Vanatta nodded. "He talked about being a Green Beret over there. Said he worked with CIA agents some of the time. That's why I half-believed the bit about a clandestine government mission. You think it could be true? Why else would he leave like that?"

Somehow, ferrying cars for Heritage Car Rentals didn't have the ring of a CIA plot. There was the occasional trip to help out old buddies from the war that might provide the opportunity for some black operation, but I'd had a little experience with CIA officers during my Air Force career, and Damon's story sounded more like the product of a vivid imagination. I was beginning to harbor other thoughts. The possibility of drug dealing first crossed my mind. I mentioned it to Jill as we left the restaurant.

"You really think he's peddling drugs?" she asked.

I opened the door of the rental car for her. "I don't know. But I have the definite feeling that Mr. Saint is up to no good. I'd like to know what really goes on in that basement workshop."

"I trust you weren't impressed by the clandestine operative story," Jill said.

I climbed in beside her and started the car. "The CIA took part in a lot of Special Forces operations in Vietnam, Laos and Cambodia. Damon Saint could have been involved in one of them. But secret agent he's not. Intelligence organizations don't turn up thirty years later and ask the help of ex-soldiers who've done nothing more sinister than clean carpets for a living."

HAPPILY, FROM MY POINT OF VIEW, the flight back to Nashville was equally as tranquil as the flight up. No doubt much of the credit went to Jill and her expertise at the Cessna's controls. At any rate, we arrived back at the office late that afternoon with a little better handle on the real Damon Saint. We found two messages on the answering machine. The last call had come in only thirty minutes earlier. Jesse Logan wanted us to get back to him at the Opryworld Hotel. The first call, recorded that morning, was delivered in a frantic whisper.

"Mr. McKenzie, this is Molly Saint. I couldn't get your cell phone. Damon said he had to go downtown, but I don't know how long he'll be gone. After he left, I got to thinking about what you said about his workshop. When I tried the basement door, I found it unlocked. He left in a big hurry. I don't know if he forgot it in the rush or if he thought I was so conditioned to staying away I'd never even consider going down there. Anyway, I figured the booby trap would be turned off. I didn't want to mess with any switches, though. So I got my flashlight and sneaked down. You won't believe what I found. Call me from a pay phone as soon as possible. I don't want your number showing on our Caller ID. When I see pay phone on there, I'll call your cell phone. Please hurry."

8

After Jill heard the message, her face went pale. "That poor girl. She sounded like she'd seen a ghost. What do you suppose she found?"

I spread my palms. "Whatever she saw, it must have been a shocker. I hope she's still at home."

I turned on the cell phone and stuck it in my pocket as we hurried out to the sidewalk that ran along the front of the shopping center. A pay phone hung on the wall two stores down. I dropped in a couple of coins, checked the number Molly had given us and dialed. After three rings, more than sufficient to trigger the ID, I hung up.

"I hope she's all right," Jill said.

"I'm sure she's okay." I didn't feel as certain as I sounded, but I didn't want to alarm Jill any more than necessary.

As we headed back to the office, I pulled the cell phone out of my pocket.

For the next several minutes, Jill sat at her desk and I sat at mine. The phone lay in front of me.

Soundless.

We both stared at it, hoping. But I heard nothing other than the hum of the refrigerator in the storage room.

Shortly, the faint wail of an ambulance siren came from somewhere out on Old Hickory Boulevard. Then silence.

Jill nearly jumped out of her chair when a car backfired nearby in the parking lot. I shook my head and glanced back at the silent phone. I had a feeling it was not going to ring. Either Molly was not at home or something had happened that I didn't care to contemplate.

I finally handed the cell phone to Jill. "I'd better call our friend Logan. Hopefully, he's ready to roll. You talk with Molly if she calls."

I punched in the Opryworld Hotel number and asked for Jesse Logan's room.

"I finally got the okay to proceed with Operation Skullduggery," he said. "If you and your wife can meet me tonight at the King Cole's in Brentwood, I'll show her what she needs to know about being a hostess."

"What time?" I asked.

"How does seven sound?"

"Fine with us. When did you figure on starting her at the Hendersonville location?"

"She can go out there in the morning and put in an application. They're short on help at the moment. She can say in the app that she formerly worked for us in the Atlanta suburbs. Let's say Roswell. The manager will have to check through my office. We'll see that she gets the job. With any luck, she can be on duty the day after tomorrow."

BRENTWOOD WAS A WEALTHY BOOMTOWN on the south side of Nashville that housed the likes of country music stars and millionaire Titans pro football players. The natives tended to be restless at mealtime and regularly filled area restaurants like King Cole's, which featured castle-like décor and moderately-priced meals. When we arrived, at least a dozen people sat or stood at the front while the hostess, a tall, slim blonde wearing a badge that read EDNA, busily wrote names on a sheet marked with columns for "# in party," "smoke," "non" and "1st avail."

I glanced about in the subdued lighting and spotted Logan coming over to greet us. He ushered us to a table near the front with a good view of the hostess station.

Turning to Jill, he grinned. "I told Edna you were a hospitality magazine writer, working on a story about King Cole's. When things slow down, you can talk to her and ask any questions you have."

After we had ordered coffee and cheesecake, Logan sat back and looked around. "This place reminds me of my first restaurant. It was in Birmingham. I was fresh out of college and signed on as an assistant manager trainee." He had a nostalgic look in his eyes.

"You've come a long way since then," I said. "How long ago was that?"

"Twelve years. I guess I've done okay for a kid from the projects who didn't play football or basketball."

As we ate our cheesecake, Logan briefed Jill on the duties of a hostess. She asked for a little more detail on her relationship with the waitresses and the manager. Afterward, she walked over to the blonde named Edna and inquired about her position and how she handled problems with customers and employees. Meanwhile, I checked the cell phone in my pocket to be sure it was still powered up. It was.

But Molly Saint had not called.

I didn't like the implication.

BACK HOME IN TIME FOR THE TEN O'CLOCK NEWS, we got an update on the murder of Dr. Elliott Bernstein. Our friend Phil Adamson turned out to be the lead investigator for Metro. Knowing his background, it didn't come as a surprise. Before becoming a homicide detective, he had won several citations as a patrol officer. I recalled what one of his colleagues had once told me, that a patrol officer does more in a week than an FBI agent does in a year. Phil had a degree in criminology and taught the subject at a tech school one night a week. On TV he sat solemnly beside the chief of police as Nashville's top cop confirmed they were deep into the process of checking hotel records and interviewing employees. The chief reluctantly admitted they were only interested in black employees, but reinforced this reasoning by showing surveillance camera videos of the suspect in the black hat and trench coat.

The first segment took place in the corridor off a balcony from which the shot had been fired. As the chief explained it, one of the Secret Service agents had looked up at the balcony when they first came in, but saw no one. When the agent heard the rifle crack, he checked back and got a glimpse of someone moving away from the railing. By the time he could run up the stairs, however, the assailant had disappeared. The video showed the man strolling toward the balcony area with one hand inside his coat. A few minutes later he hurried back in the other direction. As the chief pointed out, the murder weapon, a .22 rifle, could have been hidden inside the long coat. Unfortunately, the balcony itself was not covered by a camera, although the shooting, in the lobby below, appeared on four different videotapes.

The second taping came from a tunnel used by employees that led out to a laundry building beside an employee parking lot. But as with the other segment, the facial detail wouldn't permit a positive identification. I had an odd feeling of familiarity as I watched the videos, but had no idea why. I didn't know any Opryworld employees.

9

THE FOLLOWING MORNING, when we still hadn't heard from Molly, I called Heritage Car Rentals and asked to speak to Damon Saint.

"Damon isn't here," said the man who answered. It sounded like the black guy who had manned the front counter.

"Is he working today?" I asked.

"Probably not. He hasn't checked in this morning. Could I give him a message in case he calls?"

"Thanks," I said and hung up.

"Should we try calling Molly again from a pay phone?" Jill asked.

"I guess that's all we can do. Why don't we head for King Cole's in Hendersonville and I'll call while you put in your hostess application."

To get there, we had to take Old Hickory Boulevard around the eastern outskirts of Nashville. Fortunately, it wasn't rush hour, or the divided highway near our office could have looked like a parade of snails on wheels. The route took us past the entrance to the Hermitage, Andrew Jackson's stately homeplace, then past the big Dupont facility known as the Powder Plant after its establishment near the end of World War I. When we turned off in the Madison suburb to hit Gallatin Road, I thought about how insular some Nashvillians could be. I knew from experience that many people on the other side of the city had no concept of where Madison was, much less what might go on there. From the big shopping complex that surrounded Rivergate Mall to the county line, where Hendersonville began, the scene was a gaudy conglomeration of strip centers, restaurants, car dealers and shops.

We found King Cole's in a free-standing stone building with the same castle look we had seen the night before, surrounded by a sea of asphalt. Only a few employee cars sat in back. The restaurant didn't open until eleven. Jill went inside to talk to the manager and I walked over to a pay phone at the edge of the parking area. The weather had turned more March-like, something not uncommon in this changeable time of year. Brisk, chilling gusts swept the lot.

I dialed Molly's number and waited while it rang. I heard a beeping sound but, instead of an answering machine, got a recorded voice that said, "The number you have reached is not currently in service."

Thinking I might have dialed the number wrong, I tried again. The message did not change.

I had a bad feeling about it.

I waited in my Jeep until Jill came out of King Cole's. She had a smug look as she climbed in.

"Looks like I've got a job," she said. "If everything checks out in Atlanta, I can go to work tomorrow night."

"Great, babe. I always said you were the consummate hostess. We have another problem, though."

"What kind of problem?"

"Molly's phone is not in service."

"You mean as in out of order?"

"Or disconnected."

She looked around as she buckled her seat belt. "Why would it be disconnected?"

"I don't know, but I think we should look into it. We've had the cell phone on since late yesterday, and she hasn't called back. That's not good."

WE ARRIVED IN ANTIOCH AROUND ELEVEN. The southeastern suburb featured a middle- class assortment of apartments and condos, modest single-family homes and duplexes. Located near one of Nashville's two big lakes, it was a haven for boaters and fishermen. After checking my map, I found the Saints' street in a subdivision of small houses, most a combination of brick and wood. You could tell the owner-occupied homes by the neat lawns, many with attractive plantings in front. Others were not so tidy, some with cannibalized cars in the driveway, though a Metro ordinance expressly forbade the practice. Damon and Molly Saint's house was on a short cul-de-sac, with the back yard jammed against a thickly forested piece of property. Leaves had begun to peek out from some of the trees.

Finding no vehicles on the street or in the driveway, Jill and I got out and looked around. The house was red brick on the end that appeared to house the bedrooms and beige vinyl siding where I assumed the living room resided. The lack of a fence in back seemed to bear out what Molly had told us, that Damon had no love for dogs.

Seeing no signs of anyone around, we walked up to the small concrete porch and rang the bell. I could hear the chiming sound it made inside. No one answered.

A decrepit-looking Ford Taurus sat in the driveway to the next house, so we strolled over there and knocked on the door. The woman who opened it looked to be in only slightly better shape than the car. Rail thin, with frizzly gray hair and a forward thrust to a face that might have been related to the Grinch, she wore a loose-fitting, washed-out green housedress.

"I saw you over there looking around," she said, giving us a slow once-over. "You interested in renting?"

"Do you own the place?" I asked.

"Heavens, no." She shook her head. "Fellow named Wayne Marshall owns it. He lives across town. He's a real estate agent."

"We were looking for Molly Saint," I said.

"They moved last night."

I couldn't believe it. "They moved out?"

"That's what I said. Damon loaded up his big pickup truck last night and they left. Must have been around nine or ten."

I looked around, saw the concern on Jill's face. "Do you know where they went?"

"I didn't even know they was moving. They never said good-bye or kiss my grits. And me being so close all these years." She sounded hurt by the oversight.

"By the way," I said, "I'm Greg McKenzie, and this is my wife, Jill."

"Pleased to meet you," the woman said. "I'm Flossie Tarwater. That's Miss Flossie. Ain't never been married and don't go for that Miz stuff."

"Were you and Molly good friends?" Jill asked.

"Good as any, I guess. I wouldn't say we was bosom buddies. But we talked occasionally."

"She hadn't given you any indication they were planning to move?"

"Nope. I wasn't real sure they were aiming to move at first. He loaded a lot of stuff in the back of that pickup, but they didn't take any furniture. Didn't have a moving van, either."

"What made you decide they were really moving?" I asked.

She grinned. "I thought they might be skipping out without paying the rent, so I called Mr. Marshall this morning."

I thought it more likely an excuse for an ingrained case of nosiness.

"He knew they were moving?" I asked.

"Said Damon called yesterday. Something about his job. Said they were leaving some furniture they didn't need. The rent was paid up, though."

I couldn't imagine what about his job would necessitate a move. From what I had been told, I got no hint that he planned to leave Heritage Car Rentals.

Jill glanced back at the vacant driveway. "Was Molly in her car?"

Flossie nodded. "They put some stuff in hers, too. She drove off and he followed her in that truck."

"Was there any indication that she was reluctant to go?" Jill had a troubled look on her face.

"Reluctant?"

"Like she really didn't want to go. Did he seem to coerce her to get into the car?"

Flossie pursed bloodless lips. "Didn't look that way to me. Matter of fact, he held the door open for her. He wasn't usually that gentlemanly."

"What was their relationship like?" I asked. "Did you ever hear them yelling or fighting with each other?"

Flossie pulled her head back and frowned. "Why you want to know all these things, Mr. McKinley? Who are you?"

"McKenzie," I said, giving her one of our cards. "We've been retained to look into Damon Saint's background. We have reason to believe there could be problems between him and his wife. Have you seen or heard anything that would indicate the relationship was rocky?"

"I never saw or heard any big arguments, if that's what you're talking about. But I didn't notice much show of affection either. In recent months they mostly seemed to go their own ways."

"Not what you would have expected," Jill said.

"You're right about that, young lady."

Jill punched me in the back and I had to stifle a grin.

"In my younger days," Flossie continued, "I don't mind telling you, I had plenty of beaus that knew the proper way to treat a lady. They'd hold my hand and open doors for me. And when we was out they'd snuggle up real tight." She gave a broad grin that showed a row of teeth I'd call a dazzling gray. "I didn't have to show it all, either, like these half-dressed girls you see all over the mall nowadays. You probably wouldn't believe I'm seventy-seven now."

She was right about that. I'd more likely have guessed eighty-seven or ninety-seven. But I pretended to agree.

"So Damon and Molly traveled by themselves," I said.

"They sure did. He seemed to come and go as the spirit moved him. She worked days, of course. But some nights and weekends she'd go out with a friend. Said it was a girl she knew at work."

Flossie rattled on for several more minutes without saying anything of value to our investigation of Damon Saint. We finally eased away and left her standing there, tongue still wagging. Sadly, the current whereabouts of our client remained as uncertain as ever.

10

AFTER STOPPING FOR LUNCH AT A CATFISH PLACE, we headed back to the office. I looked up the number for Wayne Marshall and got him on the phone. I explained the gist of our interest in Damon Saint, then inquired about the sudden move.

"Damon called yesterday and told me they were leaving," Marshall said. "The ungrateful shit should have given me more warning. I've rented to him for six or seven years. He claimed he had an opportunity for a good job elsewhere."

"Did he say where?"

"No."

"Did you ask him?"

"I didn't give a damn where he was headed. He still had a month to go on his lease. He didn't have the right to break it like that."

"Did you tell him that?"

He calmed down rather quickly. "Yeah, but I didn't push it. I figured it wasn't worth the hassle. He's a cold fish you really don't want to mess with."

"I understand he left some furniture behind."

"According to what he told me. Said it was worth more than the rent. I haven't been out to see for myself."

"What do you know about his workshop in the basement?"

"I wasn't aware he had one. I guess he could have put in a workbench or something. The basement's unfinished."

"When was the last time you looked through the house?"

He hesitated. "I don't know. It's been a while. Damon offered to handle any minor maintenance. About the only thing I've had to do is put on a new roof a couple of years ago."

"In other words, you haven't been inside the house in a few years."

"I didn't need to," he said, his voice peevish.

"I'm not being accusatory," I hastened to say. Actually, I thought he was probably a pretty sloppy landlord. "Of course you had no reason to go in there. But we'd like to look at the place if you plan to check it out."

"You would, huh? I guess I ought to go out there and see what they left, especially whether they did any damage."

"That would be nice to know," I said.

"If they did, they damned sure won't get any deposit back."

"Could you meet us out there today?" I asked.

"I suppose so. I've got to see some people out that way

about a house sale at three. What time could you make it?"

"Anytime."

JILL AND I SAT WAITING IN MY BLACK GRAND CHEROKEE when Marshall drove up to the Antioch house shortly after two. The SUV had been red until a run-in with a couple of hoods in Florida back in the fall had made a new paint job necessary. I had decided black would be somewhat less conspicuous for a PI. When Marshall stepped out of his car, a gusty breeze swirled black hair splotched with gray above a round, chubby face. He looked fiftyish, with a dark suit that appeared as rumpled as the portly body it covered.

I handed Marshall one of our cards as I introduced Jill and myself. He shook my hand, then squinted through thick-lens glasses as he read the card. He shoved it into a coat pocket and pulled out a large ring full of keys.

"I don't know what you're looking for in there, but let's go see," he said. He chose one of the keys and lumbered toward the front door.

We followed him inside and found a small living room that appeared completely furnished. There was a sofa with an oval-shaped end table, an easy chair with a twisted wire magazine rack and a metal floor lamp beside it, a glass-fronted wood cabinet in one corner, no doubt designed to hold a TV set.

But I saw no TV. So I suppose the room wasn't completely furnished after all.

The rest of the house looked about the same. All of the personal items—clothing, toilet articles, jewelry, photographs (if there had been any)—were gone, but virtually all of the furnishings were still there.

"I could fix a full meal for us with this," Jill said from the kitchen.

"I should think so," Marshall said, smoothing his tousled hair. Then he grinned. "I can rent this place as a furnished house now, provided old Damon doesn't change his mind and come back after his stuff."

Despite having been rapidly vacated, the place appeared neat and clean. "Looks like a pretty good little rental," I said.

Marshall nodded. "I bought her as a HUD repo back in the eighties, after Congress screwed up the tax laws and threw the S&L's into a tailspin. HUD ran full pages of foreclosures back then. I got a good deal on it. Paid a lot less than what they were asking."

I looked into a small hallway off the kitchen. An outside door to the back yard stood on one side. Opposite it was another door.

"Does this go to the basement?" I asked.

Marshall craned his neck. "Yeah. Don't guess it's locked."

Noting two heavy-duty keyed deadbolts above the doorknob, I recalled Molly's comments about her husband's security concerns. But when I turned the knob, the door opened promptly. Wooden steps headed down, and I saw a switch plate on the wall just inside the door. Something had been removed above it and a couple of small wires dangled loosely, probably connections for the booby trap Molly had mentioned. I flipped the light switch, but nothing happened. Darkness filled the void below.

I turned to Marshall. "The power should be on. We heard the doorbell when we came out earlier."

"I told Damon to leave it on, that I'd change it to my name. The bulb must be burned out."

"I'll get my flashlight," I said.

I hurried out to the Jeep and pulled my big MagLite from under the seat. Back inside, I switched on the flashlight and led the way down the stairs. What Marshall had described as "unfinished" turned out to be a small, neat room with oak veneer paneling.

"Damn!" Marshall said, eyes widening. "I didn't know a thing about this. He was supposed to let me know if he wanted to make any alterations."

"Looks like he did a pretty good job," Jill said. "What's this?"

I shined the light where she pointed. A narrow wooden cabinet about six feet tall stood against the wall, open in front. Large hooks were screwed into either side near the top. A mirror approximately two feet square hung on one wall. Odd. Nothing else adorned the walls, like tools or posters or photographs.

"Here's his workbench," Marshall said from across the room.

I flashed the light over there and saw a wooden bench about five feet long and two feet deep, a large anvil-shaped vise mounted at one end. A two-tube fluorescent fixture dangled by chains from the ceiling. There were two wall switches just above one end of the bench. When I flipped one, the fluorescent lights flashed on.

"Voila," I said. I turned off the flashlight.

Jill looked around. "This is a nifty layout."

When I flipped the other switch, an exhaust fan that had been hidden by the light fixture whirred into action.

Marshall stared up at the fan. "Why'd he put that in, I wonder?"

I was beginning to pursue the same question. Several electrical outlets had been mounted at the back of the workbench. A couple of dark spots on the wooden surface could have been the result of heat, as from an electrical appliance. Recalling a seminar I had attended a few years back, put on by Drug Enforcement Administration agents, I suggested a possibility.

"A smart guy who wanted to set up a meth lab here would have put in an exhaust fan to suck out any toxic fumes."

Marshall turned his head. "What are you talking about?"

"The process of cooking down a bunch of ingredients such as pseudoephedrine, lye, acetone, muriatic acid and Coleman lamp fuel can produce some deadly by-products, such as phosphine."

"What the hell's phosphine?"

"Remember the Nazis' gas chambers during the Holocaust? Phosphine was one of the gases they used."

"I remember you mentioned the possibility of Damon Saint dealing drugs when we were in Indianapolis," Jill said.

Marshall glared. "Are you telling me he was making drugs down here in my basement?"

I shook my head. "I'm telling you it's a possibility. You've probably read in the paper about the big meth problem in Tennessee."

"Yeah. But I thought it was in the counties outside Nashville."

"It's anywhere. He could have made methamphetamine here using a hot plate. His wife told us he claimed to be making jewelry in the basement. But you'd expect some sort of stool to sit on for tedious work of that kind. From the size of that vise and the roughed-up look of the bench, I've got my doubts. The way he cleaned out this place, though, we'll probably never know for sure. Crime scene techs might be able to come up with some trace evidence."

Marshall looked up from the bench. "You plan to have them check it out?"

"I'm afraid I don't have access to that kind of resources."

"Could you ask Detective Adamson to check it out?" Jill asked.

"If I had something to go on besides speculation."

11

"I STILL THINK WE OUGHT TO CONTACT THE POLICE," Jill said as we drove back to the office.

"On what grounds?"

"The meth lab?"

I shook my head. "We have no proof whatever."

I had looked all around for garbage bags but found none. Damon Saint appeared to have cleaned the place out like a professional. Not surprising, I thought, considering his experience with Pro-Kleen Carpet Care. But after we had left, I thought of one place I hadn't checked—the drawers in Damon's workbench. No doubt he had looked inside, but had he pulled them out? Sometimes papers would fall behind drawers and be missed. There could be other places a more thorough probe might turn up something useful. I needed to go back for another look.

"What about that call from Molly?" Jill asked. "She obviously saw something down there that really shook her up."

"True. But, unfortunately, we have no idea what it was. Maybe drug paraphernalia. Maybe the carcass of some canine he caught."

"I didn't see any blood," she said. Then her eyes narrowed. "It was something that scared her to death, Greg. Flossie Tarwater didn't detect any coercion, but I'll bet Damon walked Molly to the car and opened the door to make certain she got behind the wheel. Then he followed her to be sure she drove where she was told to. We have to help her. There's no telling what he might do."

I finally surrendered and agreed to call Phil Adamson when we got to the office, provided Jill would rustle up a cup of cappuccino. Addicted to the stuff, we used a powdered French Vanilla mix rather than a noisy machine.

"Hi, Greg. How are you making out with the new client?" Phil asked.

"Great. Jill's going to work at the restaurant tomorrow night as a hostess. Hopefully she can dig up some leads worth following. How's the Bernstein case going?"

Adamson gave one of his patented growls. "Nothing we can hang our hats on yet. We've been interviewing hotel employees. Got a couple of black room service guys with no alibis. We have a possible motive, but haven't been able to link it to them."

"What's the motive?"

"Seems the hotel had to pass up a proposed pay hike after the Fed made a big jump in interest rates. It affected the convention business and some people got laid off."

"Interesting. It sure would have helped if somebody had seen the guy, though."

"Oh, they did. A couple of women from housekeeping passed him in the tunnel. But they didn't pay much attention, thought he was an actor dressed for the mystery party some convention was holding that night. We found a few other employees who were in the parking lot around that time, but they don't remember seeing anything."

"Are the Bureau boys giving you any trouble?" I sipped gently on my cappuccino to avoid a roasted tongue.

"Trouble! They'd like to move us out of the way, but the chief ain't budging. He says they want us to do their job with the small crap like bank robberies. He's not about to give in to them on a high profile case like this. It's supposed to be a joint effort."

"Sounds like a little turf war."

"Yeah. I don't agree with the way things are going. Sure would be nice if everybody would share what they know. It's like the old federal problem with homeland security. But the Bureau doesn't want to tell us what they're doing, so we're reciprocating."

"A typical joint effort," I said.

"We're checking out a few other things. The surveillance cameras gave us some good shots of the guy, but not a full face. He had a porkpie hat pulled down and the collar turned up on his coat."

"We saw it on TV last night," I said. "At least you've got something to go on. That's better than we've done with the Molly Saint case."

"Molly Saint? Name sounds vaguely familiar. What's it about?"

"She talked to somebody down there before she came to us. Maybe it was your office. She says she's afraid of her husband and asked us to check him out."

"Oh, yeah. That's where I heard of her. She didn't have near enough to make a case, as I recall. We told her we investigated crimes, not people's suspicions. I don't suppose you've turned up anything."

"There's definitely something wrong here," I said, toying with my cup. "We just haven't been able to put a finger on it yet."

I gave Phil a quick brief on what we had learned in Indiana, about Molly's call to us and what we had found at the house in Antioch. "Any way you might be able to help us on this?"

"I don't see how right now, Greg. We've really got our hands full with Bernstein. The chief's got everybody running their asses off. If you get something more solid on Molly, though, give us a call."

"Thanks, Phil. I will."

"By the way," he added. "I'm sure I don't have to tell you not to let out any of the stuff I've mentioned. The captain would fry me in an iron skillet."

"Don't worry. I'm an old hand at this confidentiality game. But I'm curious, why'd you decide to confide in me?"

"You're a top-flight investigator, Greg. I have a lot of respect for you. I know you get around town a lot. I figure if you have the big picture and you see or hear something we might need to know, you'll give me a shout."

After I related Adamson's remarks to Jill, I told her I didn't see what else we could do for Molly unless she got back in touch, even though we hadn't earned all the money she'd given us. We didn't charge the flight to Indiana to her account. I could probably have gotten most of the information by telephone, though experience has shown a face-to-face interview is much more productive. Anyway, Jill said she needed the flight time to get back up to speed after several idle months resulting from rotator cuff surgery.

"I think I'll call the freight line and see if Molly's there," Jill said. "Maybe she's checked in with them."

While she talked with a woman at Maxxim Motor Freight, I got on the other line and checked our answering machine at home. Surprisingly, we had a message from the manager at the Hendersonville King Cole's. He had received an okay from the Atlanta office and wanted Jill to come in tonight. The hostess scheduled to work had called in sick.

Jill frowned as she hung up the phone. "Molly took a few days off, as she told us. They've heard nothing from her."

I nodded. "Did you by chance inquire about the girl in the office who was Molly's close friend?"

"Her name is Peggy Davidson. She's an insurance clerk who works with Molly. She's in Memphis for a couple of days. Getting clued in on a new insurance carrier who's taking over the company's account. I left word to have her call me when she gets back."

"Good thing we don't need to do anything at the moment," I said. "You're wanted in Hendersonville in a little over an hour. I've got to get busy making arrangements on my end."

AFTER CONTACTING LOGAN, I took Jill home and made a few phone calls. One was to a young man I had met who was interested in learning something about detective work. I had taught him a few surveillance techniques and promised to use him occasionally. I asked him to find a good observation post around King Cole's and count the customers going in that night.

Jill left for Hendersonville in her Camry about the same time I headed out to the Opryworld Hotel.

Logan's room had a balcony that looked out over the Riverwalk area, which was several times larger than the Lakeside section. Its soaring canopy of glass covered buildings with a New Orleans look, plus a river that ran around the area with flatboats carrying passengers. Among the buildings inside the Riverwalk was one that housed the hotel's major restaurant, which had the tall white columns of an old Southern mansion. Palm trees, tropical greenery and brightly blooming flowers lined walkways along the riverbank.

After showing me the view, Logan invited me to have a seat at a round table near the doorway to the balcony.

"It's a good thing I went out to the bank today," he said. "Got all the arrangements made." He opened a leather attaché case on the table. "Here are the marked bills. Have you had time to line up your customers?"

"I'll bring a couple of parties of four," I said. "We'll have two checks for each table."

"I've counted the cash, but you'd better do it again. I want to be sure we agree."

As I thumbed through the stack of currency—twenties, tens and fives, five hundred dollars in all—I reflected on the plan I had devised. I would take the friends I had recruited out to King Cole's and have them order expensive dinners. We would pay with cash. King Cole's cash.

WE ARRIVED AT THE RESTAURANT AROUND SEVEN. I had brought Sam and Wilma Gannon, our friends whose son Tim was the victim in the murder case we had solved back in the fall. My "date" was another member of our Sunday School class, Dee Webber, a silver-haired widow whose husband had headed a local fast food firm. I let Sam sign up with Jill so she would be calling for the Gannon party instead of McKenzie.

Just behind us were two other couples from Gethsemane United Methodist Church in Hermitage. They had been briefed on what we were doing. Leading the party was a guy named Burton Pace, who was a retired deputy sheriff from just across the line in Wilson County.

After a brief wait, Jill managed to seat us at nearby tables but with different servers. As she placed the menus in front of us, she smiled at Dee.

"That's a handsome guy you've got there," Jill said. "Your husband, I presume?"

"You're not suggesting I would go out with somebody else's husband, are you?" Dee asked with a grin.

"You never know these days."

We ordered wine and steak or lobster, running up a nice tab. The rather humdrum conversation did little to liven the evening. The subject that brought the most reaction involved an effort to re-zone several parcels of property near our church from single family to multi-family, a move that would allow construction of an assisted living facility. The proposal had touched off a storm of squabbling in the area.

"Sounds like a good idea to me," Sam said. "I'll bet that section of Hermitage has a lot of folks in our age bracket. Wilma and I might be looking for a place like that before too long."

"I don't know." Dee Webber gave a slight shake of her head. "Having too many old folks around might be a bit intimidating if you're not ready for it."

"Jill keeps telling me we're only as old as we think we are," I said. "Sometimes I get the feeling she still thinks like a kid."

"That's interesting," Wilma said with a smirk. "According to Jill, you're the one who's prone to act like a kid."

There's a difference between kidding and acting, but I didn't want to get into that. Meanwhile, I did my best to keep an eye on Jill, on how she made out with her hostess chores. I noticed she frequently cast glances at the waiters, particularly when they were carrying checks.

Our server turned out to be a talkative young fellow who said he was a student at Volunteer State Community College, just up the road toward Gallatin. He did a fair job of bringing hot rolls and keeping our coffee cups filled. After we had stuffed ourselves with food and drink and dessert, he brought checks for Sam and me that each totaled more than fifty dollars.

I had arranged for Sam to sit next to me. Turning my wrist at just the right angle, I photographed the checks with one of my latest pieces of spy gear, a watch camera. The gadget was barely larger than a sports watch. It displayed hours and minutes just like a regular timepiece, but when you pressed a button, the display showed what the camera lens saw from the side of your wrist. I had provided Burton Pace with another miniature digital camera, that one about the size of a pen. Sam and I put our cash out, leaving generous tips that would require no change.

"Have a nice night," Jill called out as we left.

After taking leave of my friends at a parking lot in Hermitage, I headed home and downloaded the digital images from the watch and pen to my computer.

JILL CAME DRAGGING IN A LITTLE AFTER ELEVEN and sprawled on the sofa like a three-year-old rag doll.

"I hope you enjoyed stuffing yourself," she said, blinking tired eyes. "I haven't spent so much time on my feet in ages. I'm beat."

"I thought an old shopper like you would have no problem."

"Fighting impatient customers and waiters convinced you're ignoring them is not like shopping."

I patted her on the shoulder. "Want me to make you some coffee?"

"I don't want to even think about food or drink." Then she glanced up with a troubled look. "Have you heard anything from Molly?"

I shook my head. "Sorry. Maybe we'll hear something tomorrow. But we'd better get to bed now. Remember, we have to be at the bank when they open the night deposit bag in the morning."

12

PROMPTLY AT 8:30 A.M. ON FRIDAY, Jill and I met Logan in a private room at the bank in Hendersonville. Stacks of bills lay on the table before us. We went through them one-by-one, comparing the numbers to those on a list the bank had made up the day before. Only one twenty-dollar bill from the cash my dinner companions and I had used showed up in Thursday night's proceeds.

"Where's your photos of the checks?" Logan asked.

I took them from an envelope and laid them on the table. He had gone by the restaurant earlier and picked up King Cole's copies of the checks from the night before. He would have them back before the manager came in. We soon determined the checks for our meals were missing. However, we found other checks with the same transaction numbers in the pile, showing only pie and coffee. The difference amounted to over two hundred dollars.

"How could that happen?" I asked.

Logan had a look of disgust on his face. "The manager must have a little computer program of his own that slips in to change the data. The question is, how many are in on it?"

When he compared the checks with the head count my man had done outside the restaurant, Logan said either a lot of people got free meals or a sizeable amount of cash was missing.

Jill looked around. "I talked to one of the waiters about how much money you could make there. It was Charlie, the boy who had your table, Greg. Something he said made me wonder—wait till Sunday, that's when you can really cash in."

"The only thing different about Sunday is the buffet from eleven to three," Logan said.

I turned to Jill. "Did they ask you to work Sunday?"

"Not yet. The girl whose place I took is supposed to work tonight. I'm scheduled for Saturday."

"That's tomorrow."

"I know." She sighed. "Maybe I'll be rested up by then."

"Did they give you a rough time last night?" Logan asked with a grin.

"It wasn't all that bad," she said, fudging a bit, I'm sure. "I'm just not used to that much standing at one time."

"Why don't you try to talk to a few more waiters tomorrow night," I said. "Make them think you're interested in getting some of that extra money. See what they say."

Logan looked thoughtful. "There's one possibility I've

heard of with a buffet. You could hold out a few tickets and use them over and over again with different customers, then pocket the money."

"It's a one-price buffet?"

"Right."

"What about drinks?" I asked.

"After a few customers, you'd have whatever you needed—checks for two people, three people, with drinks, without."

I thought about that for a moment. "Don't they have the time printed on them?"

"That's right. You could tell by the time whether a ticket was old or not."

"It might be worth laying on another meal monitoring project," I said. "We still have plenty of cash left."

Jill liked the idea. "I'll bet we wouldn't have any trouble recruiting some church folks for the Sunday buffet."

"Good," Logan said. "Let's do it."

WHEN WE GOT TO THE OFFICE A LITTLE AFTER TEN, there was a message to call Wayne Marshall, the Saints' landlord.

"I thought you'd want to know," he said in a rush. "That house burned down early this morning."

"The Saints' house?"

"Yeah. With all the damned furniture and everything else inside. It was blazing big time before anyone saw it. I just came from over there. It's a total loss."

"Any idea what caused it?" I asked.

"They say there's indications it may have been arson.

Looks like it started in the basement. The investigators are supposed to go over it later. I've got insurance, of course. Thank God I have an air-tight alibi for last night." His laugh sounded forced.

Jill and I drove back to Antioch and found the house just as Marshall had described it, nothing left but a pile of rubble. Yellow crime scene tape had been strung around the perimeter. Cheating a bit, I got close enough to see that nothing in the basement could possibly have survived. Particularly not drawers in a wooden workbench. I suspected Damon Saint had made certain nobody would be searching for clues to whatever he had been doing in his workshop.

Small pieces of blackened paneling, bits of burned fabric and other scraps of material were scattered about the yard, no doubt most blown by the wind. I wandered around picking through them and found a few pieces of scorched paper with writing on them. One had some names, but not enough to help. Mostly fragments. Then I came across a scrap that had what appeared to be telephone numbers, written with a ball point pen. Two numbers were complete, all seven digits. Another had been burned away except for the last two digits.

"Do you think they might lead us somewhere?" Jill asked.

I studied the paper for a moment, considering the alternatives. I could leave it here and maybe the fire investigators would find it. But the chances were also good they would overlook such a small scrap. Where the fire started and what likely caused it would be the focus of their search. I stuck the paper in my pocket. "We'll find out."

We drove back to the office and I tried the first number.

"You have reached the Gold Curtain Dinner Theatre," a recorded voice said. "Our regular business hours are two till eleven p.m. Tickets are still available for tonight's performance. Please call back."

When I told Jill, she frowned. "I didn't get the impression that Damon was too big on cultural events. According to Molly, he wasn't much interested in going out except to a hockey game. I wonder if he was planning to take some other lady to the theatre?"

"Maybe Flossie Tarwater, only he probably wouldn't hold her hand." I put a check mark beside the number. "I'm afraid that one's not going to be much help to us. I'll call back after two, though, and see if they've ever heard of Damon Saint. Let's see who answers the other number."

When I dialed, I got a different kind of message. "The number you have called is not in service. If you have reached this number by mistake, please check the directory and try again."

Had somebody failed to pay their phone bill, or was this another hasty departure like the Saints'? I stared at the little scrap of paper with its browned and blackened edges as I gave Jill the bad news. "Looks like we drew a blank on this one, too."

She shook her head. "I presume it's things like this that drive detectives wild."

"Or wil-der," I said as I dropped the paper into the long middle drawer in my desk.

Jill crossed her arms and frowned. "What do we do now?"

"About all we can do is offer a small prayer for Molly.

Hope something falls in our lap." I checked my watch. It wasn't noon yet. "I think I'll start making some calls to line up our buffet crew for Sunday."

"Go ahead. I can't get Molly off my mind, though. I'm going over to Maxxim Motor Freight and see what I can find out about her. Maybe they've heard something."

"I doubt it," I said. "Why don't you call like you did before?"

"How many times have I heard you say if you don't know who you're dealing with, it's better to talk face-to-face. Maybe I can come up with more information this way."

I gave her a dismissive wave. "Have at it, babe. You've been learning well. And while you're there, find out what kind of car Molly drives."

THE CLOCK ON THE OFFICE WALL showed well after one, and my stomach was pushing me to start looking for a place to eat, when Jill walked in. I knew by the expression on her face she had turned up something disturbing.

"They haven't heard from her," she said. "Of course, they hadn't really expected to, since this is the last of her days off. But I got to talk to Mr. Crenshaw." She arched a finely drawn eyebrow in a sign of awe. "You should see his office. Talk about plush. I never expected that at a truck line."

"He deals with a lot more than a truck line," I said. "That's probably the headquarters for his empire."

"It looked fit for a king. Thick white carpet, velvet draperies. His desk sits up on a platform."

"The king's throne?"

"Something like that. Anyway, when I explained things to Mr. Crenshaw, he was quite anxious that we let him know anything we found out about her."

"If she's his administrative assistant, they probably work pretty close."

"Well, he gave me a look at her file. Guess what? Her name was Molly Harrison before she married."

When she paused, I looked over my shoulder. "Should I know Molly Harrison?"

"Her mother was Darlene Harrison."

Something clicked in my brain. "Your cousin Darlene?"

"The cousin I was almost as close to as a sister until you married me and dragged me away."

"Dragged?" That wasn't quite the way I remembered it, but Jill likes to paint dramatic pictures. Anyway, I recalled Darlene as the daughter of Jill's Aunt Francine, an older sister of her mother. Jill had been a teenager when her mom died. The aunt died the same year as Jill's father back in the seventies. At the funeral, Darlene had told Jill about plans to adopt a girl of around ten, the same age as her natural son, Nick.

"I only met the girl once," Jill said, "when she was twelve. That was two years before Darlene was killed in that car accident."

As I recalled, we were stationed in Germany and missed Darlene's funeral. Jill later heard that Molly was causing her father lots of problems.

"Did you get to talk to Molly's friend?" I asked.

"Peggy Davidson. No, but I left my card and asked them again to have her call me as soon as she gets back. And I asked about Molly's car. She drives a little red Nissan Sentra." Jill sat down behind her desk and reached a hand up to rub her forehead. I had seen the gesture before when she felt bogged down by frustration. "We have to do something to help Molly, Greg. I owe it to Darlene."

I moved over and perched on the corner of her desk. "Doesn't Molly's brother live in Nashville? Maybe we could talk to him and get a line on her."

Jill looked up the number for Nick Harrison and called, but got no answer.

Having no other way to turn, we took time out to eat lunch at a restaurant on the other end of the shopping center. While there we encountered Wayne Marshall accompanied by a tall blonde. She was a lot younger, a little taller and not nearly as wide. As soon as he saw us, he headed for our table. He introduced the girl as an agent with his real estate agency. Jill invited them to join us, but Marshall declined.

"I just talked to the fire department investigator a little while ago," he said. "The fire was definitely arson. Whoever did it knew what he was doing. He burned the place pretty thoroughly but didn't leave any clues to his identity."

"Did you tell them about Damon?" I asked.

"Yeah. The guy said they plan to keep looking for evidence, but they definitely want to talk to Damon, see if he has an alibi. I told the fireman I had no idea where the Saints moved to. You heard anything else of him?"

"Not a thing. I'll probably check back with Heritage Car Rentals and see if he's showed up around there."

"Maybe you ought to talk to the fire investigator. Tell him what you think."

I wasn't sure that was such a good idea. I had picked up what they would consider a piece of evidence, which now resided in my desk drawer. If they were to question me about our trip to the scene, I wouldn't like the idea of lying about what I had found. I would, of course. But I wouldn't like it.

I put all that aside when we got back to the office and concentrated on lining up my cadre of buffet diners for Sunday at King Cole's. Late that afternoon Jill finally got in touch with Nick Harrison. He had just arrived home, though he would not be there for long. A program at the school where he taught required his presence. He agreed to see us in the morning.

Just as we were about to hang it up for the day, a young black man walked into the office and looked around, then smiled and approached me. Dressed casually, as though he might have been ready to head for a nearby bar, he stuck out a large, calloused hand that suggested some type of manual labor.

"Mr. McKenzie? I'm Tony Yarnell."

His alcoholic breath reinforced the bar possibility. He looked mid-thirties, muscular, a bit overweight. I shook his hand. "What can I do for you, Tony?"

"I'm an old friend of Molly Saint's. I got something of hers I need bad to get to her. I heard you been looking for her and thought you might could steer me in the right direction."

"Who told you I was looking for Molly?"

"The nice old woman who lives next door. Said you seem to be a pretty sharp guy, you'd probably know where I could find her."

The flattery sounded insincere. "If that's the case, Miss

Flossie was a bit premature. We haven't located Molly yet. What did you have for her, Tony?"

He gave me a conspiratorial grin. "It's something real personal. I don't think Molly would want me to say."

"If you'd like to leave us a phone number," I said, picking up a pad from the desk, "we'll be happy to get back in touch when we have something."

The smile faded. "That's okay. I'm not usually where you can get me. I'll call you. Thanks."

He turned and started for the door.

"We would appreciate it if you would return the favor," I said. "Call us if you hear anything about Molly."

He glanced around before opening the door. "Yeah. Sure."

After he left, Jill's face was expressionless. "What do you make of that?"

"That is a man with a hidden agenda. And I'd like to know what it is. He lied about everything, even nice old Flossie Tarwater."

"Should we check into him?"

I lifted the phone and toyed with it a moment before punching in the number. "I hate to risk becoming an annoyance to Phil Adamson. Sure wish I could help him in some way."

PHIL RETURNED MY CALL AT HOME THAT EVENING. He said mine was the easiest question to answer he'd had all day. Tony Yarnell was a heavy-drinking part-time construction worker, part-time con man. He had been in and out of jail enough to be well known to everybody who worked there, as well as to a sizeable segment of the police force. The info might have been helpful had it given me any idea of what his connection with Molly Saint could be. But it hadn't.

13

NICK HARRISON WAS A HUSKY MAN with curly black hair and a bit of a droop to his broad shoulders. A football player in high school, he now resembled a forty-year-old out-of-shape linebacker complete with balloon tire around the middle. Jill recalled hearing from another relative a few years back that he had married his high school sweetheart, a pretty but overweight blonde. After graduation from a local college, he had gone into teaching.

Nick met us Saturday morning at the door to his modest split-level on a quiet street in Goodlettsville, a suburb on the opposite side of the county from us. He waved at Jill. "Come on in. I read a few months back about that murder you all solved down in Florida."

"Things get pretty exciting when you're married to a

super sleuth," she said, taking a seat beside me and patting my leg. We were in a sparely furnished living room with thick brown carpet, one of those spotless rooms so perfect you knew they only dared walk into it with visitors.

"Mom used to talk about how much fun you two had as girls," he said.

Jill had a nostalgic look. "I have some great memories of those days. I hated we couldn't be here for her funeral. Seems like that was fourteen forevers ago. So you're a school teacher. What subjects?"

"Social studies—history and geography. At a big comprehensive high school."

"Are the kids as bad these days as we read about in the paper?" Jill asked.

"Too many are. And I have a teenager of my own, so I get it day and night." He gave a slight chuckle. "She and my wife Zori went to Rivergate Mall this morning. Sorry you missed them."

"I'm sorry, too. I'd like to have met them. What year is your daughter in school?"

"She's a junior. I can't believe I'll soon have a daughter in college."

"Time has a habit of getting away from us," Jill said. "Which brings me to the reason for our visit, Nick. We're here about your sister Molly. Have you heard anything from her the past few days?"

He rumpled his broad brow. "I hadn't heard from her in ages until last weekend. I'm afraid we haven't been on very good terms for a long time."

"What's the problem?"

"Were you aware that my dad died about four years ago?"

Jill shook her head. "Sorry. It must have happened around the time we moved here. I didn't see the obit, and no one called me."

"Probably my fault. He had a heart attack. Took him in an instant. I guess that's the best way to go. But it pretty well put the kibosh on the relationship between Molly and me."

"Why was that?"

"I don't know if you're aware of her background before my parents adopted her."

Nick explained that Molly's birth parents had been abusive alcoholics. The state took her away from them and put her into a foster home. Her rebellious behavior had caused some real problems while in foster care. Darlene had hoped to turn the girl's life around and seemed to be making progress. But after Darlene died, Molly became more difficult. In high school she drank and smoked marijuana and hung out late. She quit school in her senior year and got a job as a waitress. After that Molly bounced around from one guy to another and occasionally tangled with the police.

"Dad gave up on her," Nick said. "When he died, I found he had written a will leaving everything to me. He specifically wrote in it that she was to get nothing. He was sure she'd just throw it away. I sold his house for enough to pay off the mortgage on this place. He had about thirty thousand in savings that I put away as a college fund for Bitsy. That's our daughter."

"I take it Molly wasn't too happy about that," Jill said.

"She flew into a rage, demanded I split everything with

her. She even threatened to have somebody work me over if I didn't. I'd heard about her new husband and didn't know if she meant him or somebody else. Anyway, I felt sorry for her, but after that I wasn't about to give her anything."

I had remained quiet, letting Jill carry the conversation up to this point. "Were you aware that Molly took a secretarial course and has been working the past few years for Maxxim Motor Freight?" I asked.

"Yeah. She mentioned that when we talked."

"We came over this morning for a very specific reason," I said. "Molly is missing."

"Missing?" He jerked his head up. "Where's Damon Saint?"

"They moved out of their house late Wednesday night," Jill said. "We haven't been able to find either of them."

We had to respect Molly's desire for confidentiality, but there were some things her brother needed to know. "Actually, Damon is the reason we're looking for her. Molly came to us last Tuesday. She asked us to do a background check on him, said she was afraid of him."

Nick's eyes lit up. "Of course. That's why she called me Sunday afternoon. She had read something in the paper about a McKenzie Investigations. Said it was run by Jill and Greg McKenzie. She wondered if that was mom's cousin. I told her I was sure it was you."

Jill's face darkened. "I had a strange feeling about her from the start. But she didn't let on that she knew who I was. I thought she'd probably run her fingers down the Yellow Pages and picked us out."

"Molly didn't mention anything to me about having trouble with Damon," Nick said. "What'd he do?"

"It was just some threats. But now that we can't find her, we're really worried."

"We have reason to believe Damon is a man with violent tendencies," I said. "If you hear anything from her, we'd appreciate your calling us immediately."

As we drove away from Goodlettsville, Jill and I talked about what we had learned from Nick Harrison. He had given us a new perspective on Molly. She wasn't just the slightly naughty unpolished free spirit she had appeared. Not only had she been a holy terror as a teenager, she had threatened her brother with bodily harm over a forfeited inheritance.

I suspected that was mostly talk. From what we knew about her relationship with Damon, it seemed unlikely she had ever seriously entertained recruiting him to work over her brother. But we now knew she was capable of things we hadn't expected. It made me wonder more about Tony Yarnell's connection with Molly. What had the young con man been involved in with her? And what other surprises were waiting to pop up out there?

"I hated to hear about that squabble between Molly and Nick," Jill said. "I don't like family feuds. We never had them on my branch of the family tree."

That was true up to a point. As far as I knew, she and her parents got along fine. But Jill's dad had never warmed to the idea of having me as a son-in-law. An astute businessman, he wasn't too well versed on the military. He thought the armed forces were peopled by guys who couldn't make it on the outside. I felt sorry for all the agony Jill went through in her efforts to get her dad and me together in some sort of harmonious relationship. Trouble was we were both too bullheaded and opinionated.

"Yeah," I said. "Wouldn't it be nice if Molly and her brother could be pals like us?"

She arched a brow. "And what does that mean?"

"Well, you've never heard of me threatening to have somebody work you over."

"Do you know why we don't have problems?"

"Somehow I suspect you're about to tell me."

"You can't get away with anything, Greg." She gave me a smug grin. "I know you too well."

That was probably true. But rarely had I tried to get away with anything. Certainly not in the realm of male-female relationships. I had been hopelessly in love with her since the day we met. I sometimes think she must have put her imprint on my testosterone glands. Like Jimmy Carter, I enjoyed a little harmless lust now and then, but I never acquired the soldierly habit of bouncing from one bed to another.

BEFORE RETURNING HOME, I decided to make another try at Heritage Car Rentals. Jill and I got there around eleven. There was no sign of the black Dodge Ram pickup out front, but Art Finley's red Corvette basked in the sun. Two men stood behind the counter when we entered, one of them the same black guy we had seen four days ago.

"Is Art in his office?" I asked.

Both of them nodded and we strolled over to the manager's door and knocked. Hearing Finley bark a loud "Come in," I opened the door and followed Jill into the office.

"Hey," Finley said, jumping up from his desk. "How's the private eye business? You still looking into my boy Damon Saint?"

"We wondered if you had heard from him in the last couple of days," I said. "He moved out of his house late Wednesday and left no forwarding address."

Finley folded his hands and tapped his thumbs. "He never mentioned it to me. Let's see, he called yesterday and said he wouldn't be available to work for a few days. Something about a problem his wife was having. Seems she'd had to take a few days off from work because of it."

I noticed Damon had not mentioned he was the cause of his wife's problem. "Did he give any indication where he would be?"

"No. I didn't ask. Like I told you before, he doesn't volunteer much." He motioned toward the chairs. "You folks want to have a seat?"

"I don't believe we have anything else to ask right now, Mr. Finley. But thanks for your help. I'd appreciate your calling if you hear anything else from him. Because of our client's interest in remaining anonymous, I can't tell you much about our investigation. But it's very important that we locate Damon and his wife."

I gave him another one of our cards and we left, still completely in the dark as to where Damon Saint had disappeared with Molly. She had led a troubled life, but I doubted she had ever faced anything remotely like this. Damon had lied about his retirement and hidden his past. He had done something in his basement workshop that terrified Molly. And though I had no proof, I was convinced he had burned the house in Antioch to hide what he had been involved in.

14

AFTER LUNCH, JILL HEADED FOR THE LIVING ROOM to "kick back" on her half of our reclining love seat. Though she enjoyed a siesta whenever she could catch one, her current excuse related to the need to rest up for tonight's session at King Cole's. While she napped, I retired to the den, where we had desks with phones and computers for each of us. The room provided as much space and looked a lot neater than our office did. I had suggested working out of our home at first. I'm not much on appearances. But Jill insisted if we intended to be professionals, we needed to look like professionals. And that meant hanging our shingle on an office door.

Sitting down, I began to type up my notes from the interviews with Nick Harrison and Art Finley. In the process, my sleeping wife missed out on the birth of a compositional pro as

I channeled my thoughts directly through my fingers into the digital world. Big deal.

When I finished, I printed out hard copies for the Molly Saint file folder. Then I transferred the computer file to a floppy disk. Next time we went to the office, I would add it to the record in the McKenzie Investigations PC. Confident that I had wrapped up the day's work, I considered joining Jill for a short nap. But before I had time to make a move, the phone rang.

"McKenzie?" the caller asked.

"This is Greg McKenzie."

"My wife wants you to drop the investigation."

A resonant bass, the voice brought visions of a radio announcer to mind, though the tone sounded more harsh than mellow. I had no doubt who was talking. "This must be Damon Saint."

"She doesn't care about the money. Keep whatever's left."

"Put her on," I said. "I'd like to hear Molly say it."

"She doesn't want to talk to you."

"Oh? Well, I'm sorry, but I can't cancel an investigation without direct instructions from the client."

"Don't give me that shit, McKenzie. If you don't butt out, you're going to experience your worst nightmare."

The line went dead.

I checked the caller ID. The small window showed UNKNOWN NAME, UNKNOWN NUMBER. I knew that sometimes resulted from a calling card, and not necessarily long distance.

I'm used to threats. They don't faze me except to occasionally make my blood boil. I stewed around for a few minutes but soon calmed down if for no other reason than the absence of anything I could do about it. However, if I had held any lingering doubts as to Damon Saint's evil intentions, they had just been neatly erased. No doubt Molly remained in grave danger. One thing the threat did was take the case out of the normal routine and place it in the category of "watch your flanks." From now on Jill and I would go armed. I began to get the feeling that Mr. Saint could turn out to be quite deadly, and I intended to be prepared if I had the pleasure of confronting him.

After what he'd done in Antioch, I considered what he might try at our home. We had taken precautionary measures following the ransacking we'd suffered something over a year ago. A burglar alarm now awaited any intruders. All of the windows and exterior doors were covered, plus motion detectors both upstairs and down. Any breach of the system would trigger an automatic call to our office and cell phones, and the police would be alerted. Thinking about Wayne Marshall's house, I was happy we had also installed a fire alarm. And if Saint arrived at night, he would be greeted with perimeter floodlights set off by motion detectors.

By mid-afternoon I decided Jill had rested long enough. I didn't want to hit her cold with the bad news, so I went in and dropped onto my side of the recliner and snuggled up against her. "Awaken, Sleeping Beauty. Prince Charming has arrived," I whispered in her ear.

She blinked her eyes open and cut them toward me. "Bug out, Prince, before I turn you into a frog."

This lady has some way with words.

"You may be interested to know I had a call from Damon Saint," I said.

She sat up with a start. "When?"

"A little while ago. He was quite brief and to the point." I told her the gist of the conversation.

"What do you think he's done with Molly?"

"I have no idea. But the man gives off bad vibes. I suggest we drop by the office and back up the files in the computer. We didn't do that yesterday, did we?"

She put a hand to her mouth. "I'm afraid not. We were in a bit of a hurry when we left. Do you think he would break into the office?"

"I think a guy who would burn down the house he just vacated would do most anything." I showed her the printouts of the interviews. "I need to take these over, too."

WITH MY BERETTA IN A HIP HOLSTER and Jill's .38 in her handbag, we arrived at the office a little after three. Everything looked normal, just as we had left it Friday afternoon. While Jill was working with the computer, I looked through my desk for a report I had pulled off the Internet concerning crime in the restaurant industry. But what caught my eye was that burned scrap of paper with the phone numbers I had picked up on the Saints' former lawn. In my rush to recruit folks for the buffet, I had forgotten about calling back to check with the Gold Curtain Dinner Theatre.

The girl who answered turned me over to the manager. I explained who I was and a hint of the investigation under way.

"A man named Damon Saint had your telephone number," I said. "I'm pretty sure he wouldn't be calling about tickets. I wondered if you might know him, why he would be calling there?"

"Damon Saint," he said slowly. "Any relation to Eva Marie? Would he be an actor?"

"I hardly think so."

After another pause, he said, "Sorry. That name doesn't mean a thing to me."

I was about ready to trash the piece of paper when another possibility hit me. Only a one and a four were left of the number that had been partly burned off. Up until now, I had thought of it as the tail end of a telephone number. But it had been written to the left of the number that was not in service. Could it be an area code?

I pulled out the phone directory and checked the list of area codes. There were eight with 14 as the last two digits. Listed alphabetically by state, they ranged from Anaheim, California to Milwaukee, Wisconsin, plus Montreal, Canada. I copied all eight of the cities and their area codes and took the sheet over to show Jill, explaining what I had in mind.

"Looks like you're going to be on the phone for a while," she said.

I dropped the list on her desk. "I have a better suggestion. Pull up our phone search web page and let's see how many would be legitimate numbers."

She tried Anaheim—714—and got nothing. Next was St. Louis—314. The search on the phone number came up with Orman's Custom Arms.

"A gun shop," I said. "I think we'd better try this one."

Returning to my desk, I dialed the number in St. Louis. When a male voice answered, I asked the obvious. "Is this Mr. Orman?"

"This is Ray Orman," he said. "What can I do for you?"

"My name is Greg McKenzie. I'm calling from out of town. Do you sell all types of guns?"

"Everything that's legal and some that's questionable," he said with a laugh. "What are you looking for?"

"To be perfectly honest, I'm looking for a little information," I said. "Do you recall having any contact with a man named Damon Saint?"

Orman didn't hesitate. "You're damned right. I had lots of contact with him back in the old days. Don't know anybody who's seen him in the last ten years though. I'm convinced the poor bastard's dead. What's your interest in Damon?"

"For a dead man, he's been stirring things up quite a bit lately. I'm with McKenzie Investigations in Nashville. His wife hired us. Damon has–"

"Wife?" Orman blurted. "That's a shock."

"Why?"

"Damon was wounded in Nam where a man don't want to get wounded. You might say he got his prick shot off. No way that character would ever satisfy a woman in bed. You sure you got the right Damon Saint?"

"Sergeant, Fifth Special Ops Group?"

"Damn, man. I can't believe this. What's he do in Nashville?"

"Shuttles cars around for a rental agency. Apparently just works when he's in the mood."

"He sure must have changed," Orman said. "Damon was always a workaholic. Had to be going somewhere, doing something. Boy didn't know how to sit down and relax."

"But you haven't seen him in ten years?"

"Been longer than that since I saw him. Haven't heard of him in ten years. Ran a carpet cleaning business in Indianapolis last I heard."

That made me wonder about something else Molly had mentioned. "I heard Damon was involved in a network, I guess you'd call it. A group of Vietnam vets who come to the aid of each other if one has a problem. Do you know anything about that?"

"No. Sounds like somebody's pipe dream. As close as we were at one time, I think I'd have known if something like that went on."

When I got off the phone, I turned to Jill with a puzzled look. "If Molly's husband is who he says he is, we've got a real dilemma on our hands."

15

I DIDN'T THINK IT WAS A GOOD IDEA to hang onto the piece of evidence I had taken from the Saints' yard, so I used a match to finish the job I had no doubt Damon Saint had begun. I copied the Orman's Gun Shop number in the little black book I carried in my pocket, then ran the area code list through the shredder. I dropped a few notes about the Orman call into Molly's file and added them to the computer. And after I had burned a CD to back up all of our business files, we headed home so Jill could get ready for work. On the way we talked about what I had learned from the St. Louis gun dealer.

"Did you get any impression from Molly that her husband lacked any of the tools necessary for a successful marriage?" I asked.

She grinned. "I like the way you put it so delicately."

"I'm trying to avoid those four-letter words you're always bashing me over."

"And I appreciate it. But, no, I didn't hear anything that would have led me to believe Damon was anything but a normal, fully functional spouse."

"From what brother Nick told us, Molly had been known to sleep around. I can't see her getting into some kind of prickless relationship."

That brought a squinch of her eyes.

"And Orman didn't make Damon sound like a guy who would sit on his duff while Molly worked," she said.

"No, he didn't."

"So what do you think?"

"I think you ought to crank up the Cessna Monday morning and spirit us to St. Louis. Let's talk to Mr. Orman and compare photos of Damon Saint."

WITH SAINT ON THE LOOSE, I didn't like the idea of Jill being out by herself, so I drove her to work. My Beretta rested out of sight in its holster, but she had to leave her .38 at home since it was illegal to carry firearms into a place where liquor was sold.

As for the King Cole's investigation, it had reached the point where I figured we could probably wrap things up tomorrow if the buffet produced what we expected. I thought it time to clue the Hendersonville police in on the likely outcome. Logan had protested over the possibility of unfavorable publicity, but I finally convinced him that he should prosecute the offenders. Simply firing people would not do the job.

Others would just take it as an invitation to come in and line their pockets for a while, then move on.

I had made the acquaintance of a Hendersonville police lieutenant during my Nashville DA days and stopped by the police station to inquire about him. Saturday night being a big night in the small town, I found him on duty.

"Greg McKenzie," I said. "Don't know if you remember me. I used to be with the DA's office in Nashville."

Lieutenant Chessly shook my hand. "I remember. You were quite famous there for a while."

"Depends on your definition of famous."

He grinned. "We had a little problem once with your boy Tremaine. Can't say he has too many admirers around here. Understand you did a little murder investigating yourself last fall."

"Right. It made me decide to get back into detective work." I handed him one of our cards.

He read it and looked up. "Your wife been a cop too?"

"No. She's new at it. But I found out on that Florida case that she has a real knack for getting information out of people, particularly women. Right now she's working on a case here in Hendersonville."

I told him briefly what we had been involved in at King Cole's.

"Why didn't they come to us?" the lieutenant asked.

"They're publicity shy. The regional guy in charge wanted to simply ease people out. I finally convinced him they needed to prosecute the folks who've been stealing from them, but I said I'd do what I could to keep it quiet. Anything you can do to help on that score?"

"You got enough evidence to prosecute?"

"We should have after tomorrow."

"Bring us everything you have," Lieutenant Chessly said, crossing his arms in a thoughtful pose. "Put it all down in writing. And we'll need somebody to swear out the warrants."

"No problem. Anything you can do about keeping a low profile?"

"With all the names and addresses, we can round them up away from the restaurant. Not much else we can do when it goes to court."

"I understand," I said. "As long as you can keep it away from King Cole's, that should minimize the problem. Jesse Logan is the guy from Atlanta. I'll have him bring everything over when we have it wrapped up. I really appreciate your help. Anything I can ever do for you, let me know."

He laughed. "Just don't let those boys at Metro get you in any more binds."

Regarding that suggestion, I thought, I would be most happy to comply.

ARRIVING HOME, I punched in the code on our keyless entry system, opened the door, turned off the alarm, and looked around. Everything appeared normal. I switched on the news, which told me more than I really wanted to know about the latest rash of wrecks and murders, legislative tax battles, guns in schools, and spring weather alerts. After shutting off the TV, I sat down with one of Robert B. Parker's Spenser novels. I had started reading them when I decided to enter the PI business, thinking I might pick up a few pointers. What I picked up on rather quickly was the Boston detective's inclination to knock his way around when more subtle efforts failed to produce the results he wanted. I could hear my partner's shrill protests if I should attempt to employ my fists so readily. Now I read Parker's books purely for the fun of it.

I was not a stranger to the physical side of the business, however. Just out of college, before entering the Air Force, I had worked a few years as a deputy sheriff in St. Louis County, Missouri. It was right after my parents died and an uncle who served as chief of deputies got me the job. Dealing with drunks and pushers and users and a variety of petty hoods, I managed to gain a liberal education in street brawling. At five-ten and a couple of hundred pounds, I more than held my own. I was also in my early twenties back then. After you qualify for Social Security, you realize you're better off depending on your brain rather than your brawn. A 9mm semiautomatic can also make a difference.

Deciding to put the brain versus brawn theory to work, I sat at my desk and reviewed what we had learned about Molly Saint's husband. He was a closemouthed loner who worked occasionally, though he appeared to have money for whatever he wanted, including a big diesel pickup. According to Julio de Leon, Damon should have arrived in Nashville with a tidy bankroll. He supposedly sold jewelry he fashioned in his basement workshop, but the room more closely resembled a meth lab than a gem factory. Also, he had left Indianapolis under strange circumstances, supposedly having been recruited for a clandestine government mission.

Damon had been with Special Forces in Vietnam and was discharged after the war, although he claimed to have retired from the Army. He had written down the phone number for his old comrade Ray Orman in St. Louis, but Orman had not heard of him in ten years. Even more odd, if Damon were the soldier Orman remembered, he should never have courted and married Molly Harrison.

Recalling Perry Vanatta's comment that Damon was always a big bullshitter, and Orman's description of him as a guy who had to be doing something, going somewhere, I had difficulty reconciling his behavior with the man Molly had married. Was it a marriage of convenience? If so, I couldn't imagine what made it so convenient. And why had he suddenly turned on Molly? Although we had no proof, I felt certain that's what had happened. Did it relate to her discovery of something frightening in that basement workshop?

When a tired-sounding Jill called at 10:30 to say she would be ready to leave by the time I could get to Hendersonville, my mind was filled with the clutter of a picture puzzle that had too many odd-shaped pieces missing and too many others that didn't match up. The only promising lead seemed to be Ray Orman. I wished we could head to St. Louis in the morning, but our main paying job required us to be out digging for a different set of answers at King Cole's buffet tomorrow afternoon.

Driving toward Hendersonville, I agonized over the fact that the case of Molly Saint had more holes in it than a five-pound block of Swiss cheese.

16

AT SEVEN A.M., I pulled open the drapes that hid the French doors leading to the deck outside our second floor bedroom. The overcast that greeted me had a murky look, not unlike the state of my mind after a night of tossing and turning. Jill, on the other hand, had hardly moved since she'd slid beneath the covers around midnight. Her dark hair still sprawled across the pillow, the rest of her a motionless lump under the blanket.

I sat on the side of the bed, stuck my hand under the sheet and fondled a spot I knew would stimulate a reaction. She flinched and looked up through narrowed eyes.

"Who do you think you are, Cool Hand Luke?"

I grinned. "How about cold hand Greg? If we're going to church, we'd better get moving."

Jill struggled out of bed and headed for the shower while

I went to the kitchen and started the coffee. On the table I saw the lined yellow pad I had written notes on after coming in with Jill around 11:30 p.m. I sat down and reviewed what she had told me on the way home.

Jill can be quite persuasive, and she had been a quick learner at this PI business while serving as an Apprentice Investigator under me. She did a real con job on her fellow King Cole's employees. During a lull period around ten o'clock, she chatted with a waiter and a waitress about opportunities to pick up a little extra cash at King Cole's. The young man told her he didn't know if she could get in on it, but some of them were making money from customer cash transactions. He said he was too chicken, but he tipped her off to several he said were more daring. The waitress advised Jill to push the buffet if she worked on Sundays. That might put her in a position to cash in on some of the profits. Though everything had been expressed rather loosely, it left the definite impression that we were on the right track.

WE ATTENDED THE 8:30 SERVICE at Gethsemane United Methodist Church, where Jill had succeeded in making me a regular after years of unsuccessful prodding while I was in the Air Force. Retirement had helped, of course. Overexposure to the seamy side of humanity had left me questioning some of the tenets of the religion I had grown up with. I had seen so many people get away with the thou-shalt-nots of the Ten Commandments that I wondered if anybody really took them seriously any longer. But the lady I lived with always managed to straighten me out. Jill McKenzie was no perfect angel, but she came as close to one as I ever expected to see.

Our pastor, Dr. Peter Trent, knew us both better than I would have preferred. He greeted us with his usual exuberance.

"It's great to see you this morning, Jill. I see you brought Sherlock with you. Is he behaving himself?"

She smiled. "You know Greg."

"I'm no worse today than yesterday," I said, "and expect to be no better tomorrow."

The good reverend laughed. "You make incorrigible seem like a nice word."

I took that as a compliment and steered Jill toward our pew. As with most church-goers, we sat in the same place every Sunday. It was not the same place we had sat on our first visit to Gethsemane Church, however. We had arrived early on that occasion and found a seat on the left aisle about three-quarters of the way back. Shortly afterward, a well-upholstered matron with a mound of white hair appeared in the aisle and stared at us with a nasty glint in her eye.

"You're in my seat," she announced.

As we scooted toward the other end of the pew, I said, "Sorry, I must have been sitting on your name plate."

Since I liked the spot where we sat now, I got up and moved into the isle to let a newcomer slide past us. The music was uplifting and the sermon reminded me of a talk I'd heard at a seminar on hate crimes, which contended that people who beat up on other people were acting out their own insecurities. The preacher didn't put it quite like that, of course. He said we should put our own houses in order first, then treat others with the same respect that we have for ourselves. Must have been a twist on the Golden Rule. I've always wondered what was in the Silver and Bronze, but maybe I'm getting Moses confused with the Olympics.

When the service was over, I tracked down our ex-deputy friend, Burton Pace, and briefed him on the buffet operation. After Jill and I reached our Sunday School classroom, I checked with my luncheon recruits during the coffee-drinking session that preceded the lesson. I quickly realized the whole exercise was a blast for them. Though I hadn't divulged all the details of what we were up to, I knew it only added to the intrigue and the appeal.

ALTHOUGH JILL DIDN'T APPEAR ON THE WORK SCHEDULE for today, we decided it would not look good for her to make an appearance at the buffet. Somebody might take it as a warning. I dropped off Jill and her best friend Wilma Gannon at a nearby restaurant before pulling in at King Cole's. I had three tables of four diners this time. Sam Gannon and I would pay as singles, the others would order as couples.

The hostess who had been ill Thursday was on duty. She highly recommended the buffet with a price of $11.95. We all obliged. I had cautioned my operatives to say nothing that would hint they were here for anything but Sunday lunch.

The couple sitting with Sam and me, John and Emma Jernigan, had a son who worked as some sort of wheel at the Opryworld Hotel. He was in what we used to call personnel but was now euphemistically known as human resources.

"David told us they're broadening the investigation on the Bernstein murder," John Jernigan said.

Pushing aside my salad plate, I nodded. "I'm not surprised. I talked to a detective friend Thursday afternoon who told me the police weren't making much headway on the case."

"David said they're now looking into the possibility that it could have been somebody with a supplier, like a deliveryman."

"I hope they can find the culprit soon," Sam said. "It doesn't look good for Nashville, a big name guy like that getting blasted right in the middle of the day. In a fancy hotel, yet. I think they should hire Greg to look into it. He did a great job of tracking down my son's murderer last fall."

I held up both hands. "Thanks but no thanks. I'll let Metro and the FBI handle that one all by themselves. I've got more than enough on my plate right now."

I didn't bother to add that I hardly thought the higher-ups in the Metro PD would be clamoring for my assistance on even the simplest case, from drunk and disorderly to breaking and entering. But as I thought about what David Jernigan had told his parents, a couple of random observations suddenly linked together. Considering that Dr. Bernstein's murderer was possibly a deliveryman, I now knew why the images of the suspect I had seen on TV seemed oddly familiar. As I recalled things like size and shape and peculiar manner of walking, I thought immediately of the gloomy Computers 'n Stuff delivery guy named Larry. Though it was a long shot, I would pass along my observations at the first opportunity.

When we had finished eating and the waiter brought our checks, I repeated my Thursday night routine with the watch camera. I had jotted down the time the waiter took our order.

The checks showed times at least an hour earlier. Seeing another waiter had dropped off checks at one of our other tables, I strolled over and chatted a few minutes, capturing digital images there also. Burton Pace would take care of the third group.

After settling with our waiter, we strolled out into the parking area and waited for the rest of our crew. They joined us a few minutes later.

"I want to thank all of you for your help," I said. "Jill and I really appreciate it."

"We should be the ones to thank you," said Emma Jernigan as her husband dug around with a toothpick. "That was a delicious meal."

Sam and I left the others and went to pick up our wives. They had been watching for us through the door and came out as soon as I stopped in front of the restaurant. Sam jumped out and opened the door for the women.

"How did it go?" Jill asked as she climbed into my Jeep.

"Just as predicted," I said. "Most if not all of the tickets were old ones. When we get home I'll download the pictures from both cameras and check the results. But now I've come across a disturbing new possibility I'll tell you about later."

17

After dropping off Sam and Wilma, I told Jill about my suspicions.

"I hadn't thought about it," she said. "But you're a lot more observant of things like that than I am."

"Admittedly, it's not much to go on," I said. "But I've closed cases on longer odds."

As soon as we arrived home, I called Detective Adamson's pager. He got right back to me.

"What's up, Greg? Something new on your case?"

"No, on yours."

"Bernstein?"

"Right. It may be nothing, but I thought I should pass it along for you to decide."

I told him what I had heard from the Jernigans and the

possible link I had made to our printer deliveryman.

"Thanks, Greg," Phil said. "We're definitely looking into that angle. We'll check this out and see if your man might have made a delivery to the hotel that day, and if he can account for his whereabouts."

Next I called Jesse Logan. He sounded relieved when I told him we had the evidence on the manager and four of his servers.

"Great job, Greg. And the cops promised to be discreet in rounding them up?"

"Right. That should keep things quiet around the restaurant. What happens when the cases go to court is another matter."

"How bad could it get?" Logan asked.

"I'd not worry too much about it, Jesse," I said. "They're the bad guys. The readers and viewers should be behind you. You're standing up for honesty and integrity. People should want to patronize a business that promotes those values."

Maybe I was being too idealistic, but I hoped I was right. I told him what the Hendersonville police wanted and that I would get everything to him by tonight.

"We're working on a really troubling case involving a young woman and a dangerous husband," I said. "Jill and I need to fly to St. Louis in the morning. We'll be back tomorrow afternoon if you need us for anything. You can call us on the cell phone if you have something urgent."

"Thanks. I'll look for you tonight."

Jill and I took the pictures and other information from the buffet operation and headed to the office. We needed to put everything together in a package for Logan and the

Hendersonville cops. It was around three o'clock when we arrived at McKenzie Investigations.

I unlocked the front door and held it open for Jill. As soon as she stepped inside, she gasped.

"Oh, God!"

I moved around her and gawked at the mess. Papers were strewn everywhere. The former contents of our desks now made the floor resemble a garbage heap. The lock had been jimmied on our filing cabinet and file folders were scattered about. Wastebaskets and the shredder had been turned over. They were empty, of course, as I always carried out the trash before leaving.

I looked around, eyes smoldering. "That bastard Saint has been here."

"I wish you wouldn't use those two words in the same sentence," Jill said.

"Sorry. But that bastard is no saint. I hope he didn't tear up our computer."

I went over to Jill's desk and switched on the computer. After a moment the box flashed on the screen asking for a User Name and a Password. He might have guessed the name (we used GUMSHOE) but I was confident he wouldn't have stumbled onto our long, randomly selected password. If he had tried the computer, this is as far as he would have gotten. I typed in the correct answers and Windows booted.

"That's one consolation," I said. "But he certainly made a mess of the place."

"Hadn't we better check around to see if anything is missing?" Jill asked.

"If anything more than Molly's file is gone, I'd be surprised."

By the time we finished gathering up everything from the floor, it became obvious that Molly's file had been taken. But we managed to account for everything else.

"Are you going to call Metro?" Jill asked.

"Why?" I said with a shrug. "We know who's been here. Nothing of intrinsic value was taken. It would just be a waste of their time and ours."

"How did he get in?"

A door in back opened onto a narrow hallway leading to an exit at the rear of the building. I only used it to carry out the trash. A cardboard box that had held some copier supplies sat next to the door, and I could tell it had been pushed aside. Finding no damage to the door or locks, I could only conclude that in addition to his other talents, Damon Saint was an accomplished lock picker.

"He came in through here," I said. "Breaking and entering must be one of his specialties. Maybe he picked that up while cleaning carpets. You know, so he could get in if the customer had forgotten to leave a key."

"Really, Greg."

"Okay. Mr. Saint is one bad customer, if not an employer. He's given us the slip, but if we keep pushing to find him, which we will, he's going to come calling again. Maybe next time we'll get lucky and meet him face to face."

"I'm not so sure I'd call that lucky," Jill said, frowning.

"I intend to be ready."

"Couldn't we ask the police to put out an APB—isn't that what it's called? Maybe they could find his truck."

"All Points Bulletin. That would be helpful, but like Phil Adamson said, we don't have enough to get them involved."

"What about this break-in?"

"Mr. Saint's been trained for special operations. I'm sure he left no prints and we haven't picked up the slightest clue to the burglar's identity. Metro won't even send an officer on something this inconsequential."

"But what about Molly? She's missing."

"She is as far as we're concerned. But both Wayne Marshall and Flossie Tarwater would say she's with her husband, wherever they moved."

"Wouldn't the fire inspectors have asked the police to locate him?"

"It's possible. But since they only want to question him, it isn't likely. At least not yet."

"But we can't just sit here and do nothing. Molly's life may be in danger."

She was sitting at her desk and I gave her a comforting pat on the shoulder. "I hate to admit it, babe, but we detectives are not omniscient. Sometimes that's all we can do—just sit and wait. Tomorrow morning, we'll board your Cessna and see if we can't pick up the trail."

18

ACTUALLY, THE TRAIL HEATED UP about an hour later while I was pecking away at the computer, getting all the King Cole's details laid out for Logan and the Hendersonville cops. When the phone rang, Jill answered it.

"Oh, yes," she said. "This is Jill McKenzie. Thanks for calling." Then she motioned for me to listen in. I picked up the phone on her desk as she mouthed *Peggy Davidson*.

"I just came into the office," Peggy said, "to catch up on a couple of things. I saw the note saying you needed to talk to me about Molly Saint. Sounded sort of urgent. You're a private investigator? What's going on?"

"Molly came to us last week," Jill said. "She told us she was afraid of her husband and wanted us to check him out. She said you were a good friend."

"Yeah. We've been buddies since I came to work at Maxxim. I really appreciate the way she's taken to my mother. Mom and I live together. She's getting up in years and has a growing problem with Parkinson's Disease. Molly treats her like a second mother, brings her little gifts, sits and talks with her."

"I understand the two of you go out a lot."

"Yeah. I enjoy her company. I know her pretty well, too, and, frankly, I'm surprised she came to you about Damon."

"Do you know if they've been having problems?" Jill asked.

"Well, she was getting awfully fed up with the way he'd been treating her."

"She mentioned he had refused to take her to a concert at the Gaylord Center."

"Yeah. That was certainly one thing that bugged her."

"What else?"

"You met her. You may have gotten the impression from the way she dresses and all that Molly's got a pretty healthy appetite for some things."

"Like what?"

"Well, like sex."

"Oh."

"I don't think she was too pleased with Damon on that score."

If Damon had suffered the Vietnam wound Ray Orman described, I wasn't surprised. But it shouldn't have taken Molly five years to reach that conclusion.

"When we saw her, Molly was definitely showing fear,"

Jill said. "I doubt that came from any disappointment over being neglected or sexually deprived. Did she talk to you about what she was afraid of?"

I had to admit Jill was becoming quite adept as an interrogator. I'd have to coach her a bit, though, on phrasing her questions so they couldn't be answered with a simple yes or no. This time it didn't matter.

"I know she thought his Army experience might have inclined him toward some kind of violent behavior," Peggy said. "He was a Vietnam vet, you know."

"We know. But she told us he had never struck her."

"I don't think so."

"Then why be afraid?"

"She was probably afraid of what he might do if..."

When Peggy's voice trailed off, Jill prompted her. "If what?"

"I don't know. Just, well..."

Peggy Davidson obviously knew something she didn't want to talk about. I didn't think it would be wise for me butt in, so I covered the mouthpiece and whispered, "Push her."

Jill spoke in a firm but calm voice. "What was she afraid he might find out, Peggy?"

"It's something very personal. I'm sure she wouldn't want me to talk about it."

"Let me explain the situation," Jill said. "Molly left a message on our answering machine Wednesday morning while we were out of town. She had discovered something in Damon's basement workshop that really shook her up. She wanted us to call her, but in a way her husband couldn't find out about it. Then we learned she and Damon had moved out of their house late that night. We haven't been able to locate her. If you know something that might explain what's going on, you need to tell us now."

There was a long pause while Peggy apparently digested all of that. Finally, she said, "Molly went down there? She had talked about doing it but never dared to. And they moved out? Didn't tell anybody?"

"That's right. And I'm sure it was not Molly's idea."

Peggy spoke hesitantly. "What I was saying—or didn't say—what I mean is Molly has been having an affair with one of our drivers."

"At Maxxim?"

"Yeah. He's a long haul driver. I think it's been going on at least a couple of months. Last week Molly told me something happened and his wife had found out about them. She was afraid of what might happen if the guy's wife told Damon."

I decided it was time for me to make my contribution. "Miss Davidson, this is Greg McKenzie, Jill's husband. We operate the agency together. We need the name and address of the driver. There's a chance he might have had some contact with Molly. For her safety, we need to find her as soon as possible."

Grudgingly, she gave us the driver's name—Mitch Grooms. He lived in Donelson, a suburb to the west of Hermitage. His wife's name was Ermine. I had always thought that name a bit highfalutin, considering the expensive white fur it brought to mind. Then somebody pointed out to me that it was just a weasel.

Peggy said she had once met the snotty Mrs. Mitch Grooms, whom she called a first-class bitch. Since I hadn't had a lot of experience with different classes of the breed, I assumed that meant the woman was not too pleasant. Evidently both Mitch and Molly had reasons for straying from the hearthside.

This added an entirely new ingredient to the equation. Clearly Damon Saint was not happy with his wife for some reason. Did it involve her relationship with Mitch Grooms rather than anything to do with his basement workshop? Maybe, but that didn't explain burning down the house. The questions continued to mount while the answers were getting almost as scarce as ermine coats at an animal rights convention.

When we got off the phone, I checked my watch. "I should have this King Cole's report finished by five," I said. "We can take it to the hotel and leave it with Logan, then have a go at Mr. Grooms."

"What if Ermine is there?" Jill asked.

"Then we just might ruffle her fur."

JESSE LOGAN GLOWED LIKE A HUNDRED-WATT BULB when he read the results of our investigation. He was so pleased he wanted to buy our dinner, and I figured it wouldn't be polite to refuse. We left the Opryworld Hotel around seven and headed home. After looking up the number, I called Mitch Grooms. Jill listened in on another phone.

A male voice answered, which I assumed was not Ermine.

"Mr. Grooms?" I asked.

"Yeah. Who's this?"

"My name is Greg McKenzie. I'm with McKenzie Investigations. Molly Saint hired us because she was afraid of her husband, and now she's missing. I need to know if you have heard anything from her in the last day or two."

"You're shittin' me, man. Did my wife hire you?"

"We got your name from Molly's friend Peggy Davidson," I said. "Molly's life could be in danger."

"I'm sorry if she's got problems, but I got problems, too. Lucky Ermine isn't here right now or I wouldn't even talk to you."

"I appreciate your situation, Mr. Grooms, but do you have any idea where Molly could be?"

"I haven't talked to her since I saw her at work a week ago Friday. Hell, my wife would have me in court if I even looked like I wanted to call Molly. Anyway, I was told Molly was off all this past week. I was on a run for four days."

This was not the most productive interview I'd had lately. In fact, it was getting nowhere. I decided to make one more try.

"Has your wife said anything that would lead you to believe she has been in communication with Damon Saint about this?"

"No. She never mentioned him. But she can be pretty hotheaded at times. She said she'd kill Molly if she ever caught her around me."

I gave him our number and asked that he call if he heard anything about Molly. When I hung up, Jill looked across and shook her head.

"Somebody else out to get Molly," she said.

"True. But I suspect Ermine is the least of her worries."

19

MONDAY MORNING WAS ANOTHER COOL ONE, but what I didn't like was the looks of the sky. Dark gray clouds cluttered my view. Something seemed to be running behind, pushing them along at an unhealthy pace. And like most of the weather around here this time of year, it came straight out of St. Louis.

"Maybe we should wait until tomorrow," I said as we finished breakfast. The radar on TV showed a mass of white stuff obscuring the map between Nashville and St. Louis.

"We can't afford to wait," Jill said. "Anyway, that overcast isn't very thick. We can get above it and fly in the sunshine."

I frowned. "Looks like a pretty stiff wind up there."

"So it'll take a little more flying time. The distance is about the same as Indianapolis. Come on, Greg. I've got every kind of instrument you can think of on that airplane. Even if we had to fly IFR all the way, there'd be no problem. Don't be such a wimp."

"Wimpiness has nothing to do with flying. It's based on a whole different set of criteria."

"Criteria, being plural, is a set."

When she starts correcting my English, I'm in trouble.

"Well, I have known some wimps who really loved to fly," I said.

"I'll get the flight attendant to serve cocktails the whole trip. You won't even know you're off the ground."

"Just be sure you have an extra-large barf bag."

I drove to Cornelia Fort Air Park, realizing this was my last opportunity to exercise some control over my destiny for an uncertain future. Jill did a thorough inspection of the Cessna, called for another check of the weather and filed her flight plan. I tried to think of some other good reason we shouldn't pursue this mission, but failed. Finally, I strapped myself in, listened to the engine roar to life, heard Jill talk a lot of pilot jargon on the radio, and we took off into what quickly became an impenetrable shroud of white.

True to Jill's word, we popped out on top after a short climb and glorious sunshine bathed us from the rear. Clumps of clouds still lurked about the sky, however, and we encountered a rash of bumps in the road. Preferring my bumps and grinds in a chorus line, I closed my eyes and pretended to doze. One thing I had learned early on was that flying does wonders for your religion. I spent most of my time uttering brief prayers.

After a span of time that seemed just short of eternity, I heard Jill request landing instructions at Lambert Field.

Opening my eyes to find we were descending through a cloud bank, I promptly closed them again. A short time later I heard the screech of tires and knew we were rolling on solid ground.

Jill parked the Cessna and we headed for the hangar to make the usual ground arrangements. The temperature was considerably lower here than in Nashville, and I was glad I had donned a well-lined jacket. After Jill finished her paperwork, we rented a car and got directions to the address for Orman's Gun Shop. Cities have a habit of changing over a forty-year span, and St. Louis hardly appeared the way I remembered it from my early days. The skyline looked different, the streets looked different, the traffic damned sure looked different.

We found the street in a suburb on the north side and followed the numbers down to a row of store fronts that included everything from shoe repairs to carpet remnants to pawn shops. Orman's was located next to a small video rental place that advertised enough X's to confuse a Roman timekeeper. We parked in front of the gun shop, which could have passed for the county jail with all the bars across its windows.

A bell jangled on the door as Jill and I entered, and though the place was not overly large, it appeared Orman had not lied when he said he stocked most any kind of gun you could ask for. Shotguns, rifles and handguns of every variety lined the walls and showcases. Ammunition boxes, cleaning kits, targets and various other accessories filled the shelves.

A man who could have been anywhere in his fifties or sixties sat on a stool behind a counter near the front. Nearly everything about him appeared gray–shaggy beard, long hair, skeptical eyes, flannel shirt. He was small but stocky, with leathery skin. The cardinal on his white ball cap provided a lone touch of color. Judging from the animal heads mounted high on the walls, he was a hunter.

"Good morning," I said with my friendly-greeting smile. "Are you Ray Orman?"

He nodded. "Sure am. What can I do for you?"

I handed him our card. "I'm Greg McKenzie, and this is my wife, Jill."

He glanced at the card, then back at me. "You called Saturday about Damon Saint. What the hell's he done to prompt you folks to come all the way to St. Louis?"

"As I told you on the phone, Damon's wife Molly hired us to look into him. He had made some threats that were quite worrisome. But before we could get very far with our investigation, she left a message on our answering machine to call her back as soon as possible. She was really excited about something. But when we tried to call, we found they had moved."

"To St. Louis?"

"I don't think so, but we don't know where. I'm hopeful you can tell us something about him that might point us in the right direction."

Orman leaned his elbows on the counter and shook his head. "Like I said, I've not heard anything of him in some eight or ten years."

"It seems about seven years ago he turned his carpet cleaning business over to the guy who worked for him," I said.

"That when he went to Nashville?"

"Apparently. He told the guy in Indianapolis he was being sent on a clandestine government mission."

"Christ. That damned boy had some wild ideas. He was a good soldier, though. I trained him."

"Are you retired from the Army?" I asked.

He nodded. "Master sergeant. I'd been saving up for a long time, bought this shop when I got out. Was you in the Army?"

"No, I retired from the Air Force. I was with the Office of Special Investigations."

"That's like CID, right?"

"Right. We were Air Force detectives. You say you trained Saint. Were you with him in Vietnam?"

"Part of the time. He was the demolition man on my team. For a while we were assigned to a Special Ops Group reconnaissance team composed of Americans and Nungs."

"What are Nungs?" Jill asked.

"It was a tribal group originally from the border area between North Vietnam and China."

"You must have been gathering intelligence," I said.

"Yeah. We did a lot of hit-and-run operations. After that they transferred us to the Phoenix Program."

"I've read some reports on that one," I said.

"I think there were lots of reports on it. A lieutenant I knew was called to testify before Congress."

"How about enlightening me," Jill said.

"We worked with what they called a PRU—Provisional Reconnaissance Unit of the South Vietnamese army," Orman said. "We were charged with rounding up and neutralizing Communist guerillas who were members of the National Liberation Front."

"And how do you neutralize someone?" Jill asked.

Orman just grinned.

"It's a euphemism," I said, "for what the CIA used to call terminate with extreme prejudice."

Jill's eyes widened. "Oh."

"The PRU's were tasked to assassinate NLF leaders," Orman said. "They would go into villages and round up anybody who looked or sounded like they might be friends of Charlie. The PRU's had monthly quotas to fill. Sometimes they went overboard."

I nodded. "The report I read said 25,000 were killed during the Phoenix Program."

"I wouldn't be at all surprised," Orman said.

"That must be what Molly was talking about," Jill said. "A driver had told her that some Vietnam vets were still causing a lot of trouble after they got home."

Orman propped his elbows on the counter. "You take a kid out of high school and teach him to kill. Then you send him halfway around the world with lethal weapons and order him to shoot anything that moves. After a year or so of that, when he's turned into a well-oiled killing machine, you send him home, cut him loose and say go find yourself a job. Well, if he tries to do what he's been trained to do, the cops ain't gonna like it. Right, Mr. McKenzie?"

"Correct. And if the people on the home front aren't too happy to see him back, that complicates things even further."

"You got that right. Fortunately, most managed to put the killing fields behind 'em. But a lot of guys got in a lot of trouble. One I know of was a buddy of Saint's who came by here recently. He spent time in Leavenworth for bank robbery. Apparently he's doing okay now. But that damned war wrecked a lot of lives."

I reached in my jacket and pulled out Molly's wedding photo. "Here's a picture of Damon made when he got married," I said, handing it to Orman.

As the bell jangled at the shop door, the old sergeant stared into the photo, his eyes bulging.

"That's not Damon Saint. That's Chad Rowe."

20

Before I could ask anything else, a new customer walked up, a tall, husky man dressed in a hunting outfit—brown and white camouflage pants, jacket and cap.

"Got my gun ready, Ray?" the man asked in a booming voice.

Orman glanced up, his face still twisted in a troubled look. "Yeah, Jeb. I'll get it. Hang on, McKenzie, be right with you."

As he walked toward the rear of the shop, the customer looked across at me. "Sorry. Didn't mean to interrupt."

I leaned against the counter. "No problem. We were just chatting."

"You one of Ray's Nam buddies? Seems like every time I come by here, he's telling war stories."

I shook my head. "I was Air Force."

"Oh. The guys who dropped the big ones."

Most of my war stories, at least the ones I could mention, were pretty boring. Anyway, I didn't want to get into a talkathon with this guy. So I merely said, "Yeah. We dropped the big ones."

Orman was back in a few moments with a slick-looking rifle that had what appeared to be a sniper scope mounted on top. He handed the gun to the man, charged his credit card and thanked him for the business.

I turned to Orman as the customer left. "What kind of game will he shoot with that?"

"He didn't say, and I don't ask a lot of questions."

"Afraid of the answers you might get?" Jill asked.

He didn't reply.

I picked up the photo. "Getting back to this, Chad Rowe as in row your boat?"

"R-O-W-E," Orman said. And, after a few moments, "He's another guy who was in my outfit. I probably shouldn't say anything else. He's had enough trouble already. I don't want to add to it."

"We think he's a danger to his wife," I said. "We need to find him before he does something to her."

"He might rough her up a little," Orman said. "Nothing worse than that."

I was getting frustrated. "He's using Damon Saint's identity—name and Social Security number. From what we found at the house he moved out of, he may be dealing in crystal meth."

"Are the cops after him?" Orman asked.

"No. We don't have enough to get them involved yet."

"So all you have is some suspicions and some guesses."

That was too close for comfort. "Well-founded suspicions," I said, "and educated guesses. What do you think happened to Saint?"

"From what you say happened in Indianapolis, I'd guess he went off his rocker and took himself out."

I stared at him hard enough to punch a hole through his skull. "I think you're making a major mistake, Mr. Orman. You could cost a young woman her life."

"Don't think so."

He had the look of a man who was suddenly out to lunch. I had been turned off completely. It was a cinch I would get no more out of him. Grabbing Jill's arm, I swung her toward the doorway. "I hope you sleep well tonight," I snapped and headed out to the sidewalk.

AS IF THE CONCLUSION TO OUR INTERVIEW had not been bad enough, the flight home was the pits. Air Traffic Control had to route us around several storms, and we wound up landing at Nashville in a pouring rain. If I'd had a security blanket, I would have crawled under it for the entire trip.

We had grabbed a bite at the airport before boarding the Cessna and really had not found time to discuss what we'd learned from Ray Orman. Having finally settled my nerves with a cup of lousy machine-made coffee at Cornelia Fort, I brought up the subject as we drove home. With the rain still pouring, the waning afternoon looked more like an early stage of evening. Taillights painted cryptic stains on the wet pavement.

"Let's see what we can fathom from Mr. Orman's performance," I said.

Jill grimaced. "He'll get no Oscar votes from me."

"The big question is, how did Chad Rowe pick up Damon Saint's identity?"

"Perry Vanatta said he sent the house proceeds to Saint at an Atlanta post office box. Maybe Rowe ran into him in Atlanta."

"We might check the Atlanta police for unsolved murders around seven years ago."

"Do you think Rowe murdered him?"

"I don't think a guy would assume another's identity unless he was damned certain the original was not around any longer."

"That scares me," Jill said.

"Why?"

"If Molly's husband has already killed an old Vietnam buddy, he sure wouldn't hesitate to kill her."

"I wonder…"

I let my thoughts wander over what she had just said. According to Orman, Rowe and Saint were both in the sergeant's outfit. He said Rowe had already had enough trouble. And he said something earlier about another buddy of Saint's who had spent time in Leavenworth.

"What are you wondering?" Jill asked.

"Remember the buddy of Saint who'd been in prison but was apparently doing okay now?"

She nodded slowly. "And you're wondering—"

"If he could be Chad Rowe. He sounded like someone

Orman would be reluctant to cause any more trouble."

"So we check Leavenworth for a former prisoner named Chad Rowe," Jill said.

"Right on, babe."

"I'll bet Phil Adamson could check that out for us."

"If he had the time, which he doesn't. See if you can get Ted Kennerly on the cell phone."

Jill left a message for him, and we were nearly home when Ted returned the call. After chatting with him for a moment, she handed me the phone.

"This Molly Saint case is really heating up," I said. "The guy who claims to be Damon Saint appears to be an ex-con named Chad Rowe. He probably did time at Leavenworth for bank robbery."

"Want me to check on him at the prison?" Ted asked.

"Right. He should have been out for somewhere between seven and ten years. I'd like to know when he was released, where he's from and where the robbery took place."

"I think I'll put my FBI friend onto it. He should be able to find the answers in their computer."

I called the office as soon as we got home to check for any messages. I found one from Grant Crenshaw, Molly's boss, requesting that we return his call. When he answered, he got right to the point.

"You've been looking for one of my employees, Molly Saint," he said. "I trust you've determined her whereabouts."

I drummed my fingers on the kitchen table. "I'm sorry, Mr. Crenshaw, but we're still working on it. We don't have anything to report as yet."

"Really? Your wife talked to me last Thursday. Surely you've heard something by now."

I didn't like his tone of voice, which seemed to question our competence. "I trust you're aware that neither Molly nor her husband told anyone where they were going. They haven't been easy to trace. But I'm sure they'll do something soon that will give us a lead."

"Well, the minute you have something, I want you to call me. I'll give you my private number. The calls are forwarded to me wherever I am."

I wasn't working for Grant Crenshaw, though I acknowledged his interest in finding Molly. From my standpoint, it had been a rather grueling day, and I didn't want to argue. So I agreed and hung up.

When I repeated the request for Jill, she tapped a finger against her chin. "He just asked if we knew her whereabouts, not if we knew whether she was okay?"

"That's right, babe. When he wasn't chastising me, I didn't detect much sentiment in his voice. He was very unemotional, sounded like his main interest was in locating her, for whatever reason."

"When I was at his office, he talked like he was quite concerned about her. He wanted to know just what her problem was, why she'd felt she had to take some time off."

Mr. Crenshaw's behavior disturbed me for some reason, and I didn't think it was just his apparent disparagement of our efforts to find Molly.

A short time later, Jesse Logan called.

"Well, they did it," he said. "The cops arrested everybody

on our hit list."

"Good. How are things going at the restaurant?" I asked.

"Smoothly. I had a new interim manager waiting, and we've augmented the serving staff from other units in the area."

"What about the hostess?" We had no evidence that the Sunday hostess was in on the take, but it looked pretty suspicious.

"I gave her the option of moving to another location or resigning," Logan said. "She quit. Thanks to the job you and Jill did, everything looks in good shape. If you ever need a reference, be sure and have 'em call me."

After I had done a replay of the conversation for Jill, she gave me a questioning look. "Then we can figure up all of our expenses tomorrow and send him a final bill?"

"Absolutely."

"So congratulations are in order, Mr. McKenzie."

I threw my arms around her and gave her a monstrous kiss. "Congratulations to you, babe. You were the heroine on this case."

She had a gleam in her eye. "I think we make a pretty good team."

"I'll drink to that," I said. "Don't we have a little champagne in the fridge?"

She brought two glasses of bubbly into the living room, where we sat on the love seat and toasted ourselves.

"Now if we can just come up with some more cases where we don't have to fly off someplace to solve them," I said.

"Actually, I was rather proud of you this afternoon. Even

with all those storms around, you didn't turn green a single time."

"I don't turn green. With all that punishment, I turn homicidal. You're lucky you're still alive."

"Don't joke about that subject, dear," she said. "I keep wondering where Molly is, what's happening to her."

"We'll find her, babe. That's a promise." I just hoped she would still be alive and well when we did.

21

TUESDAY MORNING'S NEWSPAPER carried a story, quoting anonymous police sources, reporting an African-American deliveryman for a computer store was being questioned in the Bernstein murder. The suspect was identified as Larry Inman, an ex-Marine who lived on the northeast side of town.

"Do you think he did it?" Jill asked.

I wasn't prepared to offer an opinion at this stage. I just hoped I had provided the cops with a decent lead. "If they're leaking the story, they must have more than just my speculation."

"Would Phil tell us what they've learned?"

"I don't plan to ask. He's already told us enough to get him in trouble if his boss knew about it. Anyway, I want to stay as far away from that investigation as I can."

WE HAD BEEN IN THE OFFICE ONLY A SHORT TIME when Heritage Car Rental's Art Finley called.

"I tried to reach you yesterday afternoon but got your answering machine," he said. "I hate those damn things."

"Did you have something for us?"

"A young black dude came by asking about Damon, where he'd moved to, if I knew how to get in touch with him. Stuff like that."

"The guy have a name?"

"Yeah, Tommy...or Toby. I don't remember. I didn't pay that much attention, but then I got to thinking it might be something you'd be interested in."

"Would the name have been Tony? Tony Yarnell?"

His voice perked up. "Yeah, that's it. You know him?"

"He's a local con man. He came by our office last Friday asking the same questions about Damon's wife. I trust you haven't heard any more from Damon?"

"Not a word. Of course, he's been gone like this before."

"On trips to help an old Vietnam buddy?"

"He tell you about that?"

"Right. Anyway, thanks for calling."

What was Tony Yarnell after, I wondered? Was he really looking for Molly, or was it Damon?

A few minutes later, Ted landed in the phone queue.

"The Feds came through," he said. "Warner Chad Rowe served ten years in Leavenworth for robbing a bank in a Kansas City suburb in 1980. He was released in 1991. You'll be happy to know his hometown is Gallatin, Tennessee."

"Damnation. That's great news, Ted."

"Yeah. You think that might be where he's hiding out?"

"Possibly. We'll get right on it. Did you by any chance find out who the agent was who handled the case?"

Ted chuckled. "I know you, boss. I figured that might be your next question. His name is Frank Nichols. He was a young agent back then. Now he's special agent in charge at the Memphis Field Office."

I told Jill what Ted had learned, then put in a call to the FBI office in Memphis. It took a little con job with my OSI background, but I soon had SAC Nichols on the line. I explained briefly who I was and that I was investigating a guy living under an assumed name who was actually an ex-con he had arrested at Kansas City in 1980.

"Yeah, I remember the case," Nichols said. "The son-of-a-bitch made off with over a hundred thousand we never recovered."

"Was he working alone?"

"No. He had a partner, but he refused to identify the guy. As I recall, Rowe was an ex-Green Beret from Vietnam. We suspected he was working with an Army buddy, but despite everything we tried, he wouldn't talk."

I had an idea who the buddy might have been, but I left that one alone. "How did he screw up and get caught?"

Nichols said there had actually been two bank robberies. The first one was in a small town outside Kansas City and netted only about $20,000. Rowe used part of the loot to buy a car, which he titled in his own name. Then Rowe and his buddy picked a larger bank that handled paychecks for a nearby plant. They stole a car for the getaway and abandoned it at the location where they had left Rowe's car. Someone saw them switch cars and wrote down the license number. When they heard this on their police scanner, Rowe and his buddy decided to ditch the car and split up.

"Did they split the loot?" I asked.

"No. They drove to a supermarket where they bought a bunch of plastic food storage bags. We found that out in the investigation. They also bought a small camper's shovel at a nearby sporting goods store. The clerks remembered them, but they were wearing disguises. So we couldn't get a positive ID on the accomplice."

"How did you catch Rowe?"

"They buried the cash, then headed in opposite directions, intending to meet up later and recover the loot. Rowe realized he was missing a motel receipt on which he had written an incriminating note. Thinking he had left the receipt in the car, he hurried back to the shopping center where they had ditched it. He arrived at about the same time as the police."

"You already knew his identity, if the car was titled in his name," I said.

Nichols chuckled. "Yeah, the idiot wasn't too smart in that respect. Of course, we might have considered that car stolen, too. But we would've been on his trail pretty soon. Anyway, we got lucky."

"So it looks like the partner made off with the cash," I said.

"Yeah. We confirmed it after Rowe was released from prison. We followed him to a cemetery not far from the shopping center. He dug around a grave but found nothing. When we questioned him, he gave some cockamamie story about looking for something a wartime buddy had left. The grave was actually an ex-soldier's, but not from Vietnam. We kept a tail on him for a month or so, but it didn't lead anywhere. Let us know if you find a stash of cash around him."

"Be happy to," I said. "I just hope we can find him. I'm afraid his wife's in real danger."

"Sorry I can't help on that," Agent Nichols said. "But good luck."

I hung up the phone and turned to Jill. "I think I know what happened to the real Damon Saint."

22

THE LOCAL DAILY NEWSPAPER had been my undoing back when I was with the DA's office. After making some off-the-cuff remarks about Detective Mark Tremaine at a friend's retirement party, I was shocked to find my comments splashed across the front page by a young man I had met at the dinner. Turned out he was a reporter. It cost me my job and resulted in other grief among the Nashville police that still lingered. Tremaine was from a cop family. His dad was retired from the force. An uncle was in communications, and his brother-in-law was a patrol sergeant. That no doubt accounted for a lot of my troubles with the department. But the newspaper tried to make amends, I guess, with a nice feature story a few months ago after Jill and I had solved the murder of a young Nashville architect/engineer down in Florida. The guy who interviewed us and wrote the story was Wes Knight, a veteran reporter with an unruly mop of salt-and-pepper hair and a who-gives-a-damn attitude. After we opened McKenzie Investigations, he called to say he'd like any tips we could give him on newsworthy cases.

"Hi, Wes," I greeted him when he answered the phone. "This is Greg McKenzie. How's the news business?"

"Pretty dull at the moment. This Elliott Bernstein story has some possibilities, but the most exciting thing has been the battle between the local cops and the FBI. Seems there's been a lot of wheel spinning. Maybe this deliveryman thing will pan out for them. You heard anything new?"

"Sorry, I've been too wrapped up in my own work."

"Anything I could use?"

"Not yet. But I might have something before long." I thought about the King Cole's case, but I didn't want Jesse Logan going into cardiac arrest. "I could use a little help with some background on a guy whose name I came across."

"Somebody from Nashville?"

"Gallatin."

"What did he do?"

"Got caught for a bank robbery in Kansas and did some time. It was around twenty years ago. Think you'd have something in your files?"

"Very likely. What's his name?"

"Warner Chad Rowe."

"Shad Roe?"

Shaking my head, I spelled it for him.

"Anything else you can tell me about the guy?" Wes asked.

"He's a Vietnam vet and he spent a few years in Leavenworth. That's about it."

"Okay, Greg. I'll see if we have anything. Want me to fax you whatever I find?"

"That'd be great, Wes."

"Are you in a hurry for this?"

"Actually, I am. I really appreciate your help."

"Just remember me when you break something."

"I'll remember."

I had considered the possibility of giving Wes what we had on the man posing as Damon Saint for a little speculative news story. No doubt that would shake the missing car ferryman out of the bushes, but after that threatening phone call, I didn't like the idea of his sneaking out to Hermitage and burning down our house in the middle of the night. He was obviously not a man to toy with.

"If Molly's husband tracked down his old Army buddy and killed him for taking all the bank robbery proceeds," Jill said from her desk across the way, "don't you think that's enough to warrant a call to Detective Phil Adamson?"

"If we had a way of proving it," I said.

"What if we took this wedding photo to Indianapolis and showed it to that carpet cleaner, Perry Vanatta?"

"We already know Molly's husband isn't Damon Saint. There's a possibility Vanatta may have seen Rowe with Saint, but he told us he has no idea what happened to Saint just before he disappeared."

"So there's nothing we could accomplish in Indiana."

"I didn't say that."

She came over and perched on the edge of my desk. "Okay, Mr. Detective, tell me how we could accomplish something besides sitting here on our derrieres."

"If we wanted to use a lot of your aviation gasoline and lots of our high-priced time, we could fly to Indianapolis and start questioning everybody around Saint's old neighborhood. We could also question people around his old place of business. We might turn up something, and we might not. After this many years, neighbors could have moved. And chances are those who didn't would have forgotten who they saw around Saint seven years ago."

"So you're suggesting we just sit here and wait."

I got up and sat beside her on the desk, reached an arm around her waist and grinned. "We could do a little high-powered necking while we wait."

"A little high-powered neck breaking might be more appropriate. We have to do something to find Molly, Greg. I can't stand not knowing what's happening to her."

I slid off the desk and walked toward Mr. Coffee. "Right now our best bet is to follow up on Chad Rowe. I have a hunch the newspaper files will give us some leads to pursue. Want some coffee?"

"No thanks." She moved back to her desk and sat down at the computer. "I'd better finish with this bill for Leisure Foods Group so I can get a little money to pay for our high-priced waiting."

THE FAX MACHINE BEEPED INTO ACTION about an hour later. I gathered the sheets and took them to my desk. A story datelined Kansas City, Missouri, May 2, 1980 gave details of the bank robbery and Rowe's capture. There was mention of his service with Army Special Forces in Vietnam, identifying him as a weapons specialist on an A Team. A sidebar datelined Gallatin, Tennessee, reported Rowe was a 1967 graduate of Gallatin High School. His parents lived on a small farm on the outskirts of the town, which was located a few miles from Hendersonville, where Jill had played hostess at King Cole's.

A later story covered Rowe's trial in U. S. District Court in Kansas City. According to information brought out in the trial, he had bummed around the country after Vietnam looking for a good job. But the establishment frowned on guys whose only skills were in fighting and killing. He worked at some menial jobs in the food service industry but managed to lose them, usually after a drinking spree. In the late seventies, he came up with the idea of using the clandestine skills he had learned as a Green Beret for robbing banks. The heists were carefully planned, including detailed surveillance. Rowe admitted working with a colleague but adamantly refused to give any information, even though he was offered the possibility of leniency in sentencing.

"If Damon Saint was the buddy and made off with all the loot, I can see why Rowe went after him," Jill said after reading the news stories.

I agreed. "I'd be surprised if Rowe didn't clean out Saint's bank account and arrange the house sale. The cleaning business and the house were probably paid for out of what they took in the robbery. Let's see what we can find in Gallatin."

Before we could pursue anything along that line, the

phone rang. Jill answered and handed it to me.

"This is Greg," I said.

"Mr. McKenzie, my name is Bert Quincy. A friend recommended that I call you. You may recognize the name. I'm a member of the school board and run a company called Computers 'n Stuff. Your agency bought a printer from us recently. To put it simply, I need your help in the worst way."

I had a bad feeling about this call. I hoped his use of "worst" did not prove prophetic. "What can we do for you, Mr. Quincy?"

"I have a deliveryman named Larry Inman who's in big trouble. The police are accusing him of something that is patently absurd. I need you to help me prove his innocence."

23

Quincy's office at the computer store was small but tasteful. Norman Rockwell prints on the wall, windows that probably offered a view of the parking lot masked by heavy sheers. We sat in comfortable chairs across from his tidy desk, a sharp contrast to mine, as he detailed the problem.

"Larry has worked for me the past nine years," he said. "He's an excellent employee, has never been in any kind of trouble I know of, yet they're trying to say he killed Dr. Elliott Bernstein."

I frowned, stirring uncomfortably in my chair. "Do you know what they're basing that on?"

"He made a delivery at the hotel the morning Dr. Bernstein was shot. Afterward, he stopped in a strip center parking lot to eat his brown-bag lunch, same as he always does. But, of course, he has no proof of where he was."

"Did he see anyone while he was there? Someone who might vouch for his presence?"

"No one he knew."

"I'm sure the police searched his house," I said. "Did they find a gun?"

"I'd hardly think so. Larry couldn't afford a gun. He's still paying off his mother's medical and funeral expenses."

Quincy told us how Inman had lived with his mother in the projects after his father had deserted them when the boy was fifteen. He graduated from high school in 1982 while unemployment was at high levels. Unable to find a job to help his mother make ends meet, he enlisted in the Marines. Inman was wounded in 1984 when the Marine barracks in Beirut was bombed. He was discharged four years later and found a job as a truck driver, living with his mother and helping pay their expenses. Mrs. Inman made her living cleaning houses. After a few years, they had saved enough to make a downpayment on a small frame house in a marginal section of town.

"He came to work for me when we started the business in the mid-nineties," Quincy said. "A few years later, his mother contracted viral cardiomyopathy and had to quit working. After undergoing a lot of expensive tests, she was placed on the list for a heart transplant. With all the medical expenses, they fell behind on their mortgage payments. The bank foreclosed shortly before his mother died, still waiting for a transplant. That was six months ago. Larry was forced to rent a small apartment."

I shook my head. "It sounds like he has a motive, to get back at the banking business."

"But the Federal Reserve doesn't have anything to do with mortgage foreclosures."

"In a way it does," Jill said. "The Fed establishes reserve requirements the banks must meet, and it sets the funds rate at which banks can borrow from one another. If a bank is running short, it has no option except to call in its loans, or foreclose."

"Maybe so," Quincy said, "but do you think a blue collar worker would have any idea of that?"

I rubbed my chin. "You have a point. Does Inman have an attorney?"

"He can't afford one, and I don't trust the public defender to get really excited about his case."

"So what do you want us to do?" I asked.

"Find some proof that will get the police to let him go. I'll pay your fee."

I turned to Jill. "What do you think? It could delay work on Molly's case."

"I don't like that aspect of it, but this sounds like something that would be hard to turn down."

I knew what she meant. I was certain my report to Phil Adamson was what had led to Larry Inman's predicament. From what Quincy had told us, I wasn't convinced of Inman's innocence. I also didn't want to jeopardize our relationship with Phil, but I felt a moral obligation to make certain I had not caused a gross injustice.

"All right, Mr. Quincy. We'll take the case. And we will do everything in our power to learn the truth. That's all I ever promise a client."

He nodded. "That's all I could ask. Thank you."

24

Jill was moodily silent as we drove back to the office. When I sat down at my desk, she stood there with her arms crossed.

"Why don't I go ahead with the Molly Saint investigation while you look into Larry Inman," she said.

I didn't even like to consider the prospect of her being accidentally confronted by the man we knew as Damon Saint. "I think we both need to work both cases," I said.

"Meaning you don't think I'm capable of handling an investigation by myself."

"Serendipity, babe. There's a better chance we can stumble onto something significant working together rather than separately. Let me get Phil on the phone and feel him out. Then we'll decide what to do next."

The look she gave me said volumes about my duplicitous

nature, but she sat at her desk like a stoic in marble while I called Adamson's cell phone. He had told me all the detectives used their own phones. The department provided radios, but the investigators didn't want to discuss sensitive information where all the world could listen in on their scanners.

"I understand you picked up Larry Inman," I said when Phil answered. "What did you find out?"

"Thanks for the tip, Greg. He had motive and opportunity, and his alibi is as leaky as my radiator."

"What about the gun and the black outfit?"

"We haven't found them. But he could have ditched them in a dumpster."

"I presume you've had some guys dumpster-diving."

"Yeah. No luck yet. The guy's an ex-Marine, you know. Qualified as an expert rifleman. He's got a fiery temper, too. Had to be restrained once during interrogation."

"Has he admitted anything?"

"Insists he's innocent. Nothing new there."

"Look, Phil," I said. "I have to tell you this. Inman's boss, Bert Quincy, wants us to look for evidence to prove he's not guilty."

"Oh, brother. I'd better tell you the rest of the story."

I really wasn't sure I wanted to know. "What's that?"

"Mark Tremaine is handling the Inman angle. You've got your work cut out for you, buddy. The way it looks, the guy is guilty as sin."

"If we turn up anything exculpatory, I'll let you know."

"There's something else," Phil said.

"Oh?"

"The FBI is looking into Mr. Quincy. They're concerned he might have put his boy Inman up to this."

Jill looked across at me after I hung up the phone. "What did he say that caused your hair to turn grayer?"

"Mark Tremaine is heading the Larry Inman investigation."

She nodded. "That would do it."

My critical comments about Murder Squad Detective Tremaine had involved a high-profile missing person case in which he had pursued one possibility to the exclusion of all else. My choice words about his obstinate behavior had been blown up to imply I was demeaning the entire department. Now that things were almost back to normal, I didn't relish poking in the hornet's nest again.

"I presume Phil wasn't too happy about our new client, either," Jill said.

"Probably not, though he tried to make it sound more like he only pitied us." I told her what Phil had said about the violent outburst.

She stared at me. "Sounds like something you might do in similar circumstances."

"I might," I said. "But, fortunately, I'm not being grilled by Mr. Tremaine. Phil mentioned one other complicating fact, though."

"And that would be...?"

"He says the FBI is interested in the possibility that Quincy might have talked Larry Inman into committing the murder."

"Really, Greg."

"My feelings exactly. Let's go check out where Inman lived and see what his neighbors have to say."

THE DELIVERYMAN OCCUPIED one side of a brick and vinyl-siding house in an area a mile or two off Old Hickory Boulevard that was block after block of nearly identical rental duplexes. Some looked neat enough to be featured in a homes magazine, while others could have passed for junkyards. Inman's lay somewhere in between, with a few scraggly shrubs in front and a clean lawn. Quincy had given us a key to the place, which Inman had given him in case of an emergency, and we let ourselves in.

"He's not much of a housekeeper," Jill said, noting papers scattered about the floor around a small table in the living room.

I took in the area with a quick glance. "More likely the work of a cadre of untidy detectives."

"What are we looking for, Greg?"

"The police have already carted off anything of evidentiary value. I'd just like to get a feel for the guy, how he lived, what he valued."

We found pictures of Inman the Marine, Inman and his mother, and Inman with an attractive young woman. A Bible lay on the bedside table. The place where he had been reading was marked with a laminated obituary chronicling his mother's death. A pair of ticket stubs from a movie theater had been dropped on the floor among the debris from the cops' search.

"Looks like there may have been a girlfriend," I said. "Let's see what we can learn from the neighbors."

Nobody was home in the other side of the duplex, so we tried the house next door. A young black woman in bright red capri pants balancing a small child on her hip answered the door. The tot eyed us suspiciously. I introduced Jill and myself.

The woman gave her name as Lakeesha Echols. I asked if she were acquainted with her neighbor.

She nodded. "I know Larry. He must be in big trouble."

"Did you see the newspaper story this morning?"

"No. But I seen the cops haul him away."

"Well," I said, "we've been hired to help him. What did you see over there?"

"After they took him away in the police car, them crime scene people spent a lotta time in there. What'd he do?"

"We don't think he did anything wrong, Lakeesha. By the way, do you know if Larry had a girlfriend?"

"I met her once, but she don't live around here."

"Do you know her name?"

"Franny something. Said she works at a shoe store in the mall at Rivergate."

Lakeesha didn't provide much else of interest except she had never seen Inman with a rifle or heard him mention guns. He was a nice guy who talked a lot about his mother but never said anything about banks. As usual, I gave her one of our cards and asked that she contact us if she heard anything else.

As we turned to leave, I noticed a small black Ford pickup, probably a Ranger, passing slowly down the street. The tinted windows masked whoever was inside. I tried to catch the tag number, but it was too far away. Probably nothing, but I had an odd feeling about that vehicle.

Back in the car, Jill looked around at me. "Rivergate is on the way to Gallatin. Or better yet, we could catch it on the way back. It's one o'clock. Let's grab a bite of lunch and head for Sumner County."

She wasn't about to let up on the search for Molly, and I couldn't blame her. As for Larry Inman's case, the cops needed to come up with something more solid before the DA would jump onto it. We had made a start on our investigation on his behalf. The next move would have to wait while we got back to the more pressing question of where were Molly and Damon Saint/Chad Rowe?

25

Our first stop was the Gallatin Public Library. A small structure hardly larger than the branch library we frequented at home, it was located some distance out of the downtown area that was centered around the county courthouse. A helpful young woman directed us to a shelf that held a long row of Gallatin High School annuals. I scanned the spines until I found the year 1967.

"Think Chad Rowe was a football player?" Jill asked.

"We'll soon find out." I laid the book on a table and thumbed through some of the photo pages. No Rowe appeared in the picture captions. Football or otherwise. Finally turning to the seniors section, I flipped toward the back until we found him.

"Doesn't list any extracurricular activities at all," Jill said.

The photo was of a pretty ordinary-looking teenager, short hair, solemn face. The eyes had an intensity about them that reminded me of Molly's observation that Damon seemed to be seeing right down to her soul.

"I wonder if we could find a teacher who remembers him?" I said, studying the picture.

"It's been over thirty-five years, but we could try. I saw a mention in the front of the book about a teacher sponsor or dedication, something like that."

Looking back, I found the photo of Miss Hannah Ullery, a history teacher. She didn't look too young in 1967, so I wasn't all that hopeful she'd still be around. But I looked up the school number in a phone book and called on the cell phone.

"This is Greg McKenzie from Nashville," I told the woman who answered. "I'm looking for Miss Hannah Ullery. Would she still be teaching there?"

"Oh, no," she said. "Miss Ullery retired several years ago."

"Do you have any idea where I could find her?"

"I think she's living in a nursing home. Let me ask somebody."

She came back shortly with the good news. "They say she lives at a place called Pleasant Grove Manor. It's an assisted living facility not far from the county library."

We got more specific directions from the librarian and headed out to the Jeep. After passing a row of homes both vintage and modern, we came to a rambling brick structure set back in a broad green lawn dotted with the brilliant white blossoms of Bradford pear trees. Islands of leafy plants surrounded by red and white blooms flanked the building. It did appear to be in a pleasant grove.

Sturdy furniture from an earlier era filled the bright lobby, where a dark-haired woman wearing half-glasses greeted us. "Can I help you?"

"We're looking for Miss Hannah Ullery," I said.

"Is she expecting you?"

"No. They referred us to her over at the high school. We're from Nashville. We wanted to ask her if she remembers a student from back in the sixties."

She looked over the glasses. "I'm sure she does. Miss Hannah is a sharp lady. At ninety she sometimes forgets who she was with in recent months, but she can tell you all about things that went on back at that school."

I gave her a business card, and she told us to wait while she checked to be sure the elderly resident wasn't napping. After a few minutes, she ushered us down a gray tile corridor to a door with the retired teacher's name beside it.

A large woman with short white hair, wearing a simple black dress, Hannah Ullery sat in a padded wooden chair beside a small desk. The room also had a folding table, three other chairs and a large, stuffed bookcase.

She held out a wrinkled hand. "Please pardon me if I don't get up. It's become such a chore."

We introduced ourselves, shook hands and took chairs across from her.

"I appreciate your agreeing to talk with us," I said, looking around. "You have a nice apartment here."

"Hmph." She frowned. "It's not much, but I guess a relic

like me hardly needs more. Ellie said you want to know something about a former student. I've had hundreds, probably thousands. Which one?"

"I hope you can remember him. The name is Chad Rowe."

She pursed pale lips. "Him I remember. He in trouble again?"

"You know about his robbery conviction?" Jill asked.

"Everybody in Gallatin knows about it. Well, maybe not everybody, but everybody who was around in the eighties. I wasn't surprised."

"Was he a trouble-maker in high school?" I asked.

"Not as much as some, but he had a mean streak."

"What did he do?"

"He liked to torment the girls. And I heard he would do sneaky things to the boys, too, like hiding their clothes in the locker room."

That sounded more like teenage pranksterism.

"We didn't see his name listed for anything in the annual," Jill said. "Did he play any sports?"

Miss Ullery leaned an elbow on the desk and rested her head against her hand. "No. Chad Rowe wasn't a team player. He was a loner in school. I don't remember but one boy who was friendly with him."

"Do you recall anything about his parents?" I asked.

"His daddy was a dirt farmer. I think the Rowes raised a little tobacco. According to the stories I heard, his parents were quite strict. As I recall, he came to school a few times with bruises on his arms and legs. I don't know if he was abused or not, but these days somebody would probably have called Human Services."

I decided to follow up on one comment that had possibilities. "Do you remember the boy's name who was Chad's only friend?"

She nodded. "Roger Langley. Good boy. He lived on a farm next to the Rowes. He didn't have much upbringing, but he rose above it. He's a lawyer in Gallatin now. He even drops by occasionally to call on a crotchety old schoolteacher. Come to think of it, seems I heard him say he'd had some contact with Chad in recent years."

26

WITH THE SUN MAKING ITS WAY slowly behind the old Sumner County Courthouse, I wasn't sure if Roger Langley would still be in his office. That's where we found him, though, on the second floor of a decrepit building near the square. A tall, lean man with touches of gray contributing to a distinguished look, he invited us to take seats across from his uncluttered desk.

After introducing ourselves and handing him a business card, I got to the reason for our visit.

"Miss Hannah Ullery told us you were the only friend of Chad Rowe she could remember from his high school days."

Langley frowned and toyed with a pencil on his desk. "Bad Chad. He didn't have many friends in those days, that's for sure. Probably still doesn't. Do you know where he's located now?"

I explained about Molly and our attempts to find her. "Anything you could fill us in on him would be helpful. What was he like back in the old days?"

"He could be nice when he wanted to be, but that wasn't too often," Langley said with a smile. "Personally, I never had any problems with him, but a lot of others did. He wasn't the type to fraternize. He could get in trouble in the most outlandish ways, too, like shooting at a neighbor's dog."

Jill cut her eyes toward mine, undoubtedly recalling Molly's story of the dog and the machete.

"I lived on the next farm down the road from Chad," Langley said. "It was strictly rural back then. Matter of fact, it hasn't changed a lot since. Most of the good farmland closer in has been developed for homes. I guess our old section has too many rocks and creeks."

"Did Chad have brothers or sisters?" I asked.

"No. His parents always sort of kept to themselves. They were pretty strict disciplinarians. Some of Chad's conduct was probably acts of rebellion."

"Did you have much contact with him after you graduated from high school?" I asked.

"Not much. When he came home after Vietnam, he wanted me to head off with him on some wild trip around the country. I was in law school then and wasn't interested. He said he had a Vietnam buddy who might go with him. I'm certainly glad I turned him down. A few years after that, he got caught in a bank robbery and was sent to prison. I suppose you knew about that."

"A newspaper story about it led us to Gallatin. Have you

heard anything from him since then?"

Langley leaned back, locking fingers behind his head. "A few years ago, mustn't have been too long after he got out of prison, he called me from somewhere with a weird legal question. He wanted to know if he committed a crime at the request of a government agency, could he be prosecuted."

"Did he say what kind of crime or what agency?" Jill asked, no doubt recalling the letter Perry Vanatta told about receiving from Louisville.

"No. I told him if he didn't want to wind up back in Leavenworth, or some other federal facility, he had better leave it alone. The kind of government agency that would make such a request would deny any knowledge of him if he were caught."

"I'd have to agree with you there," I said. "Have you heard anything from him since then?"

"No, but I've been trying to locate him for the past year or two. That's why I asked if you knew where he lived. His parents died and he's the sole heir to the family farm. It's been vacant for so long the old farmhouse is probably falling down. If he doesn't claim the place before long, the county will take it for back taxes."

After getting the address of the farm, we thanked Langley for his time and headed for the Jeep.

"Are you thinking what I am," Jill asked, "that Chad and Molly could be holed up in that old farmhouse?"

"It's a good possibility." I held the door open for her. "Let's go have a look."

THE HOUSE SAT A COUPLE OF HUNDRED FEET off a forlorn country road that curved downhill just past the farm. Its tin roof shone faintly beneath an early evening moon. Pairs of tall, narrow windows looked out like some strange animal eyes as we drove by. No lights could be seen anywhere about the place. A rutted dirt drive angled back on the far side of the house, beyond the crumpled remains of a metal gate.

"It looks deserted," Jill said. "Do we dare pull in?"

"Let's ease around the curve, and I'll walk through the woods to check in back," I said.

When we were out of sight, I pulled off the side of the road and parked.

"Get out your .38 and hold it in your hand," I said. "If anyone comes around, make them keep their distance. I'll be back in a few minutes. Should anything happen, call me on the cell phone."

We carried the phones to keep in communication when we were separated. I put mine on vibrate before getting out. I closed the door softly, then hiked toward the house. The terrain angled uphill and, as Langley had pointed out, was quite rocky. I took care to avoid any hidden obstacles, dodging clumps of oak, a few maple trees and an occasional cedar. The wooded area seemed dark enough that I doubted I could be spotted from the house, should anyone be inside. But when I reached the point where I could see behind the place, I found no vehicles. No lights were visible in back or in front.

I hurried back to the Jeep, turned it around and pulled up to the driveway. Then I drove to the rear of the house, where we would be out of sight of the road. We got out and looked around.

"Somebody was here recently," I said. "Look at the tire tracks."

Whoever it was had followed the same route I took, parking in back.

"Are we going inside?" Jill asked.

"If we can get in."

I got out my flashlight and shined it around the yard in back. The tall grass lay like twisted yellow wires. Aside from a few rusted farm implements, I saw nothing but a dirt-coated shovel leaning against the house and a pile of small chunks of coal nearby. I walked over to the door, noted the shiny new lock, and tried the knob. It turned and rusty hinges screeched as I pushed the door open. Directing the flashlight inside, I swept the room with its narrow beam. The house had definitely deteriorated, though it did not appear as dilapidated as Langley had suggested.

"Looks like the place has been in use," Jill said, pointing to the kitchen table, where a couple of paper plates lay beside a half-empty box of plastic forks.

"Yeah. Things are generally a mess, though. Doesn't look like they bothered with too much clean-up."

A large green garbage bag sat in one corner. A vintage electric range stood along one wall. Shelves lining another held dated utensils. An old coal-fired Warm Morning heater sat to one side, vented through the roof with a blackened pipe. We moved into the living room, which was sparely furnished. Frayed throws covered an old sofa and two chairs. One of the two bedrooms appeared to have been occupied recently, but there was no clothing around. The bathroom had been cleaned.

"Do you think it was Molly and Chad?" Jill asked. She rubbed her hands in a nervous gesture.

"I'd say it's a bit far out for the homeless." I rechecked the rooms, examining the new locks on the outside doors. "From what we saw in Antioch, Chad is adept at handling locks. This is probably his handiwork. Since there were two plates on the table and the bed appears to have been occupied on both sides, that points to Molly being with him."

"And alive," Jill said.

"Right. And considering he left the back door unlocked, I'd guess he isn't planning to return."

"What about the garbage bag over there? He disposed of the trash when they left Antioch."

I glanced about the room. "I suspect he didn't count on anybody coming around this place, at least not anytime soon."

Jill shook her head, eyes downcast. "And he's given us the slip again."

27

AFTER A FULL DAY OF WORKING TWO DIFFERENT CASES, Jill decided we deserved something special. She headed for the kitchen as soon as we got home and started working on one of her culinary delights, pork tenderloin baked in a mixture of wine and sauces. I had just sat down with a yellow pad to make notes on the day's activities when the phone rang.

"Mr. McKenzie, this is Lakeesha Echols."

"Hello, Lakeesha. What do you have for us?"

"I just heard something that might help Larry," she said.

"Great. What is it?"

"A bunch of Mexicans live in the house next to me. They work over at Opryworld. Only one of 'em speaks much English. He told me when they heard about Larry getting arrested in this murder thing, they found out one of the guys had seen this black hat, black coat guy they showed on TV."

"You mean he saw the man at the hotel the day of the murder?"

"Yeah. Saw him in the parking lot. He hadn't said anything before 'cause he didn't understand what it was all about. He's seen Larry around here, and he says it definitely wasn't Larry."

"Do you have the Mexican boy's name?"

"It's Pedro Rodriguez." She gave me the address where he lived.

"Thanks loads, Lakeesha. You're a jewel."

Jill came into the living room with her spatula in hand. "What was that about?"

"Hopefully we have a big break in the Larry Inman case." I told her what I had just learned.

"Are you going to call Detective Tremaine?"

"I have a better idea. This gives us a good opportunity to score some points with Wes Knight."

She broke out in a wide grin. "Mmm, mmm. You are one sneaky sneak."

I got Wes at the newspaper. "I have a little tip I think you'll like," I said. "But I don't want to be identified with it."

"No problem. What've you got?"

"You mentioned this deliveryman, Larry Inman, they're holding in the Bernstein case."

"Yeah. Your old buddy Tremaine is touting him as the killer."

"Well, guess what," I said, "there's a Mexican employee at the hotel who saw the shooter in the parking lot that day. He lives near Inman and knows him. He says Inman was definitely not the guy."

"No shit! Why hasn't he come forward before now?"

"The guy doesn't speak English. He didn't understand what was going on." I gave him the name and address.

"Thanks, Greg. Anytime you need anything, let me know."

When Wes hung up, I dialed Bert Quincy and told him what I had done.

"You don't think you should have called the police?" Quincy asked.

"I think this will do the job better. When it's plastered across the newspaper, Larry stands a better chance of having his reputation cleared than if it were handled by the police."

I knew from experience how Tremaine would doggedly hang onto any lead he had, rejecting the possibility that he might be wrong.

"Yeah, I see your point," Quincy said. "Do you think they'll let him go soon?"

"I would hope so, but don't hold your breath. Strange things can happen in the justice system. Have you had any contact with the FBI?"

"A couple of agents came by the store and talked to me."

"Were they only interested in Larry, or did they have some questions for you?"

"They talked mostly about Larry, but I got the impression they might be digging for something deeper. What's going on?"

When I told him what I had heard about the Bureau's interest in his possible complicity, he was flabbergasted.

"That's unbelievable. Where did they—"

"Don't let it worry you, Bert," I said. "Hopefully this new

angle we turned up will get the wolves off both you and Larry."

"I certainly hope so. And thanks for the job you've done, Greg. Send me a bill for your services."

"I appreciate the compliment, but let's wait until we're sure this thing is over."

If it turned out like I hoped, I would almost hate to send Quincy a bill. He had given me the opportunity to redeem myself for what appeared to be a bad miscalculation. Of course, Larry wouldn't be cleared unless the cops accepted the Mexican's assertion that the man he saw definitely was not the deliveryman they were holding. Still, I had begun to feel a bit smug about it. That is, until I turned back to my note pad and started recording our efforts on behalf of Molly Saint. That's when I realized we were essentially back to square one. It was Tuesday night, and we had no more idea where Damon/Chad had taken her than when we'd first determined she was missing six days ago.

28

PEDRO RODRIGUEZ' SOLEMN FACE with its down-turned black mustache stared at me from the front page of Wednesday morning's newspaper. According to Wes Knight's story, Rodriguez saw the killer getting into a car in the employee parking lot. The hotel banquet setup worker was walking between two cars one row over from the man in black. Interviewed with the help of his English-speaking housemate, he said he got a good profile look at the man's face from no more than ten feet away. In contrast to Larry Inman, whose nose was broad and flat, the man he saw had a long, narrower nose.

Rodriguez didn't know much about cars, American or otherwise, but said the one the man entered was dark green and looked new. Knight wrote that he had notified Metro's

Homicide Division about the young Mexican's sighting. After he had obtained everything he wanted, I'm sure.

"Here's the story," Jill said. I looked around where she stood beside the TV that rested on a wall bracket in the breakfast room.

A newsman was talking in front of the house next to Lakeesha Echol's. The camera cut to a dark-skinned young man with a thin mustache.

"Pedro, he very tired," said the Mexican. "Police question him all night. Get no sleep. He have to go work this morning, then police say they talk more. He no want be bothered, please."

The reporter appeared back on camera. "The police have issued no statement regarding this development, but a police spokesman promised something later this morning. That's all for now from Hillandale Street."

The anchor went on to another story, and Jill turned down the volume. She looked across at me, lips pursed. "Obviously they haven't said anything yet about releasing Larry."

"No. I think I'll call Phil and see what he can tell us."

I thought I'd have to leave a message, but, surprisingly, he answered the phone.

"Phil, it's Greg," I said.

His voice sounded weary. "I've been going for most of the last twenty-four hours," he said. "If you're looking for any more help, buddy, I'm fresh out."

"I won't bother you for long. But my client wants to know when his man will be turned loose, considering what's happened overnight."

"That newspaper guy said he got an anonymous tip. You

haven't been making any anonymous phone calls, have you?"

I laughed. "Come on, Phil. You know I'd be happy to provide Detective Tremaine with any help I could."

"Yeah. Tell me about it."

"Actually, we were out in that neighborhood yesterday and talked with a girl who lived next door to Larry. We didn't know about the Mexicans then. I just saw on TV that you interrogated the guy until this morning. Did you come up with any better description of the car?"

"Not much. We're gathering pictures from dealers and plan to bring him back in later today. See if he can identify what he saw. I don't like going through interpreters, but it's the best we could do."

I held out my cup for Jill to pour a little more coffee. "Well, I sure hope you can come up with enough to give you a decent lead."

"Don't we all. It's a good thing you called now. I'm ready to get a little shut-eye and I plan to turn off this damned phone."

"Don't blame you. But you didn't answer my question about Larry Inman. Is Tremaine causing a problem?"

Adamson grunted. "Tremaine is a problem. I told him we'd have to release the guy unless he could come up with something more conclusive. Everything he has is circumstantial. Let's see what comes out of this Mexican hat dance."

"Fair enough, Phil. Go get some sleep."

OUR CAR RENTAL BUDDY ART FINLEY called me at the office around nine. I think he had begun to like this role of detective's informant.

"In talking to one of my boys this morning," Finley said, "I learned he'd been approached by this Tony Yarnell dude after the guy quizzed me."

"One of your drivers?"

"Yeah. He's another ex-military type. Served in Korea after the war but got the hell out of the Army before Vietnam."

"That would make him around my age. What did Tony want?"

"Same questions he asked me, about where Damon might have gone."

"I presume your driver didn't know?"

"He didn't. But he gave the guy an interesting tip. I thought it might be something you'd like to know."

"What sort of tip?"

"Percy—that's the driver's name—rode with Saint a lot. I think maybe he was sort of a father figure to him. Don't really know. Anyway, Percy seemed to get more out of that close-mouthed fella than anybody around. Seems they were jawing over a few beers not long ago about the need to get away from their wives now and then. Damon mentioned this out-of-the-way motel. Said it was one he found handy when he got tired of listening to his wife's bitching."

"What motel was it?"

"The Old Country Inn. Percy said it was just off I-24, not far into Rutherford County."

That put the location a little south of Nashville on the way to Murfreesboro, home of Jill's alma mater, Middle Tennessee State University. After I hung up, I looked around to find her busily filling out a bank deposit slip. A couple of clients who had hired us to do some pre-employment checking over a month ago had finally come through. Good thing. I was about ready to shift into my nasty-letter-writer persona.

"Guess what," I said. "Damon Saint has been known to patronize a motel down in Rutherford County."

"Oh?" She tilted her head at a quizzical angle. "Recently?"

"Right. According to one of Art's drivers. At any rate, we'd be wise to check it out."

"He wouldn't be using his own name," Jill said.

"Hardly. He's not dumb."

"And he won't look like that photo from the wedding."

"Right again. I'll check back with Art and see if he might have a photo."

When I got Finley on the line, he told me he had a copy of Damon's driver's license, complete with photo. In Tennessee, we seniors didn't have to stand in line to get our pictures snapped, but the guy who called himself Saint wasn't old enough. Art said the license had been issued about two years ago. The insurance company required him to get a copy whenever one of his drivers received a new one.

As soon as Jill had finished updating her accounting program, we headed to the bank to drop off the deposit. She promptly called my attention to the sky, which had decided to twist itself into a shadowy mass of gray to the northwest, the direction from which cooler air usually invaded the area.

"Looks like a cold front about to bump into this warm air," she said. "We'll probably get some thunderstorms out of it."

I switched on the radio to see if I could locate a weather forecast. What I caught instead was the tail end of a news bulletin about a "breaking story."

"...and the young man who made headlines today had only been in Nashville about six months. He lived with several other Mexican immigrants in the duplex on Hillandale Street. Neighbors report a small black pickup truck, a stretch model, was seen leaving the area at a high rate of speed just after the shot was fired. We'll have more on this breaking story as soon as it becomes available."

Jill looked around, a confused frown on her face. "A shot fired?"

"Hillandale," I said. "A young Mexican who made headlines today? Makes it sound like Pedro Rodriguez has been shot. Let's get over there and see what we can find out."

I swung onto Old Hickory Boulevard and sped toward Madison. The location wasn't too far away. With the help of a few shortcuts I had learned in driving about the area, we made it to the duplex subdivision in around ten minutes. Several marked police cars were parked in the street, and I saw at least two plain white Malibus. Crime scene tape had been stretched around the front yard and up to the house.

I parked as close as I could, and Jill and I walked toward the tape. I didn't know any of the uniforms, but I saw a homicide detective I knew. Unfortunately, he was talking to Murder Squad Detective Mark Tremaine.

The guy who had caused all my trouble was short and stocky with a glued-in-place sneer. I knew he had solved his share of crimes during twenty years on the force, but I suspected a sizeable number had come from lucky breaks, like witnesses who appeared out of the blue with pertinent information. His tendency to jump to conclusions on skimpy evidence and cling to them doggedly, to the exclusion of any other possible avenues of investigation, hadn't helped.

Tremaine looked around as we walked up. "What the hell are you doing here, McKenzie?"

I forced a smile. "Doing my usual thing, detective. Looking for information."

"And what makes you think we'd give you any?"

"I believe in sharing," I said. "That's why I told Phil Adamson about my suspicions regarding Larry Inman."

He gave me his normal sneer. "A lot of help you were."

"I wasn't in a position to determine the truth. I knew that was your department."

"Did you ever stop to think your screwing around could get somebody killed? Like this Rodriguez boy?"

That answered my question. The Opryworld Hotel employee was dead.

"And how did I become responsible for that?" I asked. "You aren't implying Inman did this? He's still in jail."

"How do I know the shooter wasn't working with him? Anyway, while you had us off chasing after this Inman character, somebody else was out here stalking our witness."

This guy was too much. "I understood yesterday you were one hundred percent sure Inman was the killer."

"Not the first time you got your damn facts all wrong, McKenzie." His face was starting to flush. "You'd better stick to your divorces and insurance claims."

I took a deep breath. "For your information, detective, we don't do divorces."

"Well, whatever you do, stay the hell out of my way."

I turned away from him and spoke to the homicide guy, whose name was Hargreave. "Is Phil on his way over?"

He shook his head. "Phil must have his phone turned off. I've been trying but can't get an answer. I haven't been on duty long, but he was at it all night. I hate to have to tell him about this."

"Know what you mean," I said. "This was his most promising lead. Do you know what Rodriguez was shot with?"

"A seven-point-six-two round. We—"

"Don't tell him shit," Tremaine said, growling at Hargreave.

I took a step toward him, staring down at his twisted face. "Why don't you get out your magnifying glass, Sherlock, and go look for some clues."

Jill, who had remained silent until now, grabbed me by the arm and gave it a sharp yank. "Let's get going, Greg. We have more important work to do."

As I looked around at her, a black car screeched to a stop nearby and two somber young men came striding toward us. Before surrendering to Jill's tug, I glanced back at the Murder Squad detective.

"Okay, Tremaine, here's your chance to teach the FBI how to solve these tough cases."

As we approached my Jeep, Jill spoke in a soft but determined voice. "I don't believe you particularly helped our cause with that little diatribe, Greg."

I let my shoulders slump. "Sorry, babe, but that bastard deserves all the abuse I can heap on him."

"What happened to that promise to clean up your act?"

I had recently renewed my vow to cool the blue language, but people like Tremaine made it a real challenge. "I'm trying," I said.

"Then try harder."

While trying to think of a comeback to that, I saw a pickup truck move slowly down the street. Two women inside craned their necks to see what the cops were up to. The truck was small and green, but it reminded me of what the reporter had said earlier in that radio breaking news report. Neighbors had seen a small black stretch model pickup leaving the scene at a high rate of speed. As I thought about it, I realized the Ford Ranger I had seen driving down the same street yesterday when we left Lakeesha Echols had been an extended cab model. Could the neighbors have seen the same one this morning? Maybe, but yesterday no one knew about Pedro Rodriguez. Did they?

29

WE PICKED UP WHERE WE LEFT OFF and headed out Murfreesboro Road to Heritage Car Rentals, where I obtained a copy of Damon Saint's driver's license. Then we headed down I-24 toward Smyrna, location of the Nissan plant. I wondered if that was where Molly's red Sentra had been built.

We had no trouble with the traffic, but the day had taken on a bleak, almost wintry look, especially with most trees barely starting to leaf out. Rain began to spatter on the windshield before we got past Hickory Hollow Mall, where a stream of shoppers cruised in for the spring sales. I grinned at the nostalgic look Jill gave them. Shopping was her favorite sport. But instead of bargains, she saw mostly industrial sites and warehouses dotting the area along the way to Smyrna. We had just passed Sam Ridley Parkway when I spotted the billboard advertising the Old

Country Inn, "where a restful night awaits the discriminating traveler." I noted the exit and directions to turn right.

A green wall of tall pines hid the motel from the road just off the interstate. Except for a large sign pointed toward it, we might have missed the place. I could see why Chad Rowe had found the location to his liking.

A blue roof topped the U-shaped white frame building. Early-blooming spring flowers painted splashes of red and yellow that outlined the office in front. Through a small gap in the structure, I saw a swimming pool in the open area behind the office. Room wings stretched back on both sides.

When I started circling the place, we saw Chad's black Ram pickup backed against a low rail fence at the back. Beside it sat a small red Sentra.

Jill's face darkened. I had thought she would be delighted to see Molly apparently here. That wasn't her only worry.

"What are you going to do, Greg? You agreed Chad's a dangerous man. Do you think it wise to go knocking on his door?"

"In the first place, we don't know which room they're in," I said.

"So we check with the front desk?"

"Right. With his driver's license in hand."

The rain pelted the car now, creating nearly as much of a din as a waterfall. I pulled under the canopy near the REGISTRATION sign and we got out. Though we had seen a dozen or so vehicles parked around the room wings, this obviously was not a busy time of day. The office appeared empty except for the clerk. Walls and woodwork followed the blue-and-white theme. A counter stretched across one side of the room. On the other, a sign indicated the small area of tables and chairs accommodated the free continental breakfast. Behind the counter stood a smiling young woman, tall, thin and blonde.

"What can I help you with?" she asked.

I showed her the license. "Can you tell me what room this man is in?"

She glanced at the sheet, frowning. "Let me check. I don't think we have a Damon Saint."

"He's probably not using his real name," I said.

She looked back at me. "Are you a police officer?"

I gave her a business card. "We're private investigators. We saw Damon's truck and his wife's car parked in back. See if you recognize the face."

She stared at the photo for a moment. "That looks sort of like Mr. Casey. I haven't seen much of him, but he's been here a couple of days."

"Have you seen his wife?" Jill asked.

"No. Just him. He hasn't been in for breakfast that I know of."

"What room is he in?" I asked.

"We're not allowed to give out room numbers," the woman said, sobering. She pointed to a phone on the counter. "I can ring the room for you. Take the call on that phone."

I weighed my options for a moment. If I got Chad on the phone, he would not likely tell me anything to indicate the room location. In fact, he would probably do nothing but make more threats. And though I wanted to know for certain

Molly was with him, her car in the lot tended to indicate she was. A phone call would tell me if they were in the room, but I didn't want to make it with the clerk listening.

"Thanks for your help," I said, shoving the license back in my pocket.

I took Jill's arm and we walked out.

"What's next?" she asked.

I opened the car door for her. "Let's drive around back, then I'll make a phone call."

As I put the Jeep in gear and started around the motel, Jill gave me her don't-be-coy-with-me look. "And who will you be calling?"

"I saw you pick up a card in there," I said. "Does it have the Old Country Inn's phone number?"

She glanced at the card as I eased to a stop in sight of the rear of the building. I took out the cell phone and punched in the number as she read it out. When the clerk answered, I asked for Mr. Casey. I listened as the hollow ringing sound repeated itself over and over like an echo across a rock-walled canyon.

I finally closed the cover. "No answer."

"So they've gone somewhere without their two vehicles?"

I stared at the pickup and the red Sentra. "Looks like it. Maybe he rented another one, thinking these are too hot."

"Why would he think that? Who's looking for him besides us?"

"Good point. You stay in here and keep dry while I have a look at Damon's truck."

"Gee, it's nice to have a partner willing to do the dirty work."

I gave her a look and pulled in beside the big Dodge Ram. Using the red and green Fuji Film umbrella we had bought one rainy day in Jerusalem on our Holy Land tour, I walked around to the back, where a heavy blue tarp covered the truck bed. A stranded steel cable looped through the grommets, threaded into rings on the sides of the truck. A large padlock secured it at one point. I tried to pry up the tarp enough to see inside but got only a glimpse of cardboard boxes. Locks also fastened the lid of a heavy metal chest anchored near the cab.

Jill looked around as I lowered the umbrella and jumped inside.

"He didn't intend for anyone to get nosy, did he," she said.

"No. And whatever is in Molly's car has been well covered, too." I had gazed through the windows but saw nothing other than a blanket spread across whatever lay in the back seat.

The cell phone rang and I answered it.

"Greg, this is Bert Quincy." The subdued voice told me he was not in a happy mood. "Have you seen the news about that Mexican boy?"

"Yes," I said. "It appears to be a blow to Larry's case, but look at it from the other angle. The circumstances also indicate that somebody else was afraid Rodriguez might identify the real killer."

"I just talked to the police. They don't have any plans to release Larry."

"Detective Adamson told me this morning they'll have to turn him loose unless something more incriminating turns up."

"I don't like this a bit," Quincy said. "Please call me if

you hear anything else."

"Don't worry. You'll be the first to know."

Jill looked at me as I turned off the phone. "Bert Quincy?"

"Right. He may not be as eager to pay us as he was last night."

"Surely they're not going to hold Larry after what happened this morning."

"You heard Tremaine. He'll try to think of some reason, to spite me if nothing else."

"What about Phil Adamson?"

I flipped the phone open. "Maybe he's back on the job. Let's see."

I called his cell phone and got him.

"Are you over at Hillandale?" I asked.

"Yeah. How damned unlucky can we get?"

"Pedro Rodriguez wasn't too lucky, either."

"Very true. I had no idea anything like this might happen. If we could've just gotten a line on that vehicle in the parking lot. How many new green cars do you suppose are driving around Nashville?"

"Hundreds," I said. "Isn't this enough to get Larry Inman released? He sure as hell didn't kill the guy."

"As soon as I can get Tremaine calmed down, we'll see. I heard you tangled with him over here earlier."

"It wasn't my idea. We traded a few barbs, but I don't know that anybody won."

"Well, try to steer clear of him in the future. As a favor to me."

That merited a chuckle. "I'll be most happy to comply, Phil. But I'd really like to know when you're ready to do something about Inman. His boss just called again."

"You can tell Mr. Quincy the FBI is off his case. That should make him happy."

"Thanks. I'll do that."

"I'll get back to you on Inman. Right now I'm looking into a new angle that just cropped up. I can't imagine how it relates, but we'll have to track it down and see. It involves somebody you know."

"Another of my friends in trouble?"

"If you want to call him that. You asked me the other day about that jailbird Tony Yarnell. An informant overheard him in a bar a couple of nights ago, loaded as usual, bragging about his prowess as a hit man."

30

"Do they think Yarnell had something to do with this Rodriguez murder?" Jill asked when I repeated the conversation.

"I'd say it's a long shot. I'd sure like to know why he came to our office looking for Molly, then went to Heritage Car Rentals asking about Damon Saint. Lucky for us Tony got that driver to recall hearing about this motel."

She glanced across at the parked vehicles. "I gather you didn't find anything of value around those?"

"I jotted down the license numbers. We can use that to trace them if necessary."

Checking my watch, I looked back at Jill. "It's about noon. Let's go park in the far corner and set up a little stakeout."

"We're going to wait for them to come back?"

"That's the idea. Of course, we have no way of knowing when that will be. Stakeouts aren't the most exciting things a detective does, but that looks like our only option."

As the raindrops continued their frantic dance on the asphalt, we drove to a corner of the lot that bordered on a heavily wooded area. I backed against the fence, giving us a perfect view of the room doors and the two vehicles parked across from them.

"Too bad we didn't bring our books to read," Jill said after a few minutes of fruitless watching.

"That would violate the rules. I suppose we could take turns reading, but one of us needs to keep an eye on the target."

She slumped down into the seat. "If you say so."

"Come on, babe. If you're going to be a PI, you'd better get used to the weary and boring parts of the job."

"Hmph. I certainly didn't get into this for the glamour."

"Hey, I thought you looked knockdown gorgeous all dressed up for that hostess role at King Cole's."

She cut me a look, then shook her head. "Just assure me that we're going to find Molly here, or somewhere, good as new."

I thought of the familiar old contract clause "no warranties expressed or implied." I didn't feel up to making any guarantees on Molly Saint's safe return.

After I called Bert Quincy to give him the good news about his being dropped off the FBI's radar, I commented on the nasty weather and got a worried look from Jill.

"I hope they've checked to make sure my Cessna is tied down properly at the airport. I've been thinking about the possibility of renting hangar space. What do you think?"

I gave her a noncommittal glance. "The company plane is your department, babe."

That prompted a smile. "Glory be. You're admitting the airplane is a real asset to the business?"

"It helped on this case," I said. "I'm not admitting anything else."

She clucked her tongue and settled back in the seat. After half an hour, she dozed off. Another hour later, my eyes had tired of staring through what remained of the rainstorm, now only a gray drizzle. The rear of the motel continued to appear lifeless as a cemetery plot. The cell phone broke the monotony.

"Mr. McKenzie?"

"Yes."

"This is your alarm monitoring station. We have a burglar alarm in Zone One."

The front door. "Have you notified the police?"

"That's my next call."

"Thanks."

I snapped the phone shut and started the car. "Somebody's broken into the house," I said.

Jill sat up with a start. "When?"

"Just now. That was the alarm company. They're calling the cops."

I sped past the motel office and turned toward the interstate. The rain had all but stopped now, though the pavement was still wet. That didn't slow me as I raced up I-24 to the Bell

Road exit, cursed the traffic signals around Hickory Hollow Mall, and darted through traffic on our way to I-40. From there it wasn't far to our place in Hermitage.

I skidded to a stop in the driveway around two o'clock. A Metro patrol car sat there, the officer writing his report. I hurried over as he lowered his window.

"What did you find?" I asked.

"You must be Mr. McKenzie."

"Right. The alarm company called us on the cell phone. We were a little below Smyrna."

The cop—his badge said Wilcox—checked his watch and grinned. "You must've set some new speed records getting here. When I arrived, your pushbutton lock looked okay, but the front door had been bashed in. I checked upstairs and down, didn't find anybody. I couldn't tell that anything major had been taken. But it's pretty obvious somebody has a real problem with you."

My blood pressure had begun rising as he described what he had found, but that last remark kicked my curiosity into high gear. "What kind of problem?"

"Well, sir, they spray-painted one of your walls with—" He paused to check his notes. "Says, 'I warned you butt out. Next time you're done.'"

For a moment I stared, dumbfounded. Then it hit me. I turned to Jill, who had walked up just in time to hear Officer Wilcox's description of the break-in. "Damon Saint," I said without thinking, still trying to get used to his real name, Chad Rowe. "That's the same words he used before. 'If you don't butt out, you're going to experience your worst nightmare.'"

"What did he mean by 'next time you're done'?"

"My goose is cooked, I would think."

"If you know who did this," Officer Wilcox said, "I'd advise you to go down and swear out a warrant against him."

"Thanks. I appreciate your help. Do you need anything else from us?"

"No, sir. But I'd say you need to find you a good housepainter."

As soon as we opened the door, Jill gasped at what she saw. The entrance foyer gave a view of the stairway up to the bedroom level at the left, a look into the living room on the right. Red spray paint on the living room wall ran down in places like trails of blood.

"That's horrible," Jill said. She shook her head, almost in tears.

I wasn't always the greatest of help, but she took pride in keeping the house in mint condition, neat as a military barracks ready for inspection.

"Don't worry, babe," I said. "I'll get somebody onto it right away."

"It isn't just the paint, Greg. It's the message. What do you think he might do, and what has he done to Molly?"

"I intend to find out." I sat on the sofa and picked up the portable phone from the end table, punched in Phil Adamson's number. When he answered, I said, "This is Greg again. We found Damon Saint."

"Your client's husband? Was she with him?"

"I think she is, but I'm not sure. Actually, we found where he's staying, at a motel off I-24 below Smyrna. Both his truck and her car are parked there. I couldn't get an answer at the room."

"Any idea where he's gone or when he's coming back?"

"No. But I know where he's been." I told Phil about the break-in and the spray-painted warning. And I gave him a brief rundown on Molly's husband's real identity?Chad Rowe.

"Shit, man, sounds like you're dealing with a real nut case."

"It's beginning to look that way. The motel clerk wouldn't give out his room number. I wondered if you had any contacts in the Rutherford County Sheriff's Office?"

"I didn't until today. I've been on the phone a couple of times with Investigator Tune about a body they found this morning. They identified it as Tony Yarnell, the character who bragged about being a hit man. Saves us from looking for him any longer."

"What happened to him?"

"His throat was slit and his body was thrown off a bridge. Come to think of it, they found him near Smyrna."

"When did it happen?"

"The preliminary report says sometime last night. He shoots his mouth off about being a hit man, then he's the one who gets hit. Must be some kind of poetic justice."

"They have any idea who did it?" I asked. Jill had snuggled up against me, trying to hear the conversation. I cocked the phone away from my ear a bit so she could listen in.

"One reason Investigator Tune called me was to get some help," Phil said. "He got my name from another deputy who's a student in my criminology class. Seems Tony Yarnell had a card in his pocket with several telephone numbers. Two of them were home and work numbers for an employee at the Metro jail."

"That's interesting. Who's the guy?"

"It isn't a guy. She's a clerk Tony would probably have had access to during his many visits to the jail, courtesy of the courts."

"What's her name?"

"Ermine Grooms."

I felt Jill stiffen at his mention of the name.

"I have to tell you this, Phil," I said, "Ermine Grooms is the wife of a driver at Maxxim Motor Freight, where Molly Saint works. During our investigation, we learned that Molly recently had an affair with Mitch Grooms, the husband. When I talked to Grooms last Sunday, he said Ermine had threatened to kill Molly if she caught her around him."

"Damn. Tony had a pocketful of cash when they found him. You don't suppose this Ermine hired him to kill your client?"

I thought about it a moment. Could that have been Tony's reason for coming by our office, for asking Art Finley about the man called Damon?

"Maybe she did," I said. "Tony talked to one of the drivers who worked with Chad Rowe at Heritage Car Rentals. The guy told him about the motel where Rowe's staying. That's how we found out about it. Maybe Tony went down there looking for Molly but ended up tangling with Chad instead."

"Give me the name and location of that motel, Greg. I'll contact Investigator Tune and see if he can meet us down there."

"Have you got time to do that? What about the Bernstein case?"

"I'm looking for any excuse to get out of here. This place is going crazy. The Bureau boys are all cranked up over the Rodriguez shooting. One of the neighbors identified the shooter's vehicle as an extended cab black Ford Ranger. The FBI is out shaking the bushes for it. I sent Tremaine off to be our liaison with them. Let me call Tune and I'll get back to you."

31

I DID A QUICK PATCH JOB ON THE FRONT DOOR, and Jill tried to clean the offending red message off the wall while we waited to hear from Phil. The paint was probably a quick-drying enamel. It refused all of her efforts. She finally gave up and fixed cappuccino, which we drank at the kitchen table.

"I know Molly sounded a little off-the-wall at first," she said, her forehead wrinkled in despair. "I agreed with you that just being a Vietnam vet didn't make her husband the demon she cast him as. But now this, after what we learned about Chad Rowe."

"I just hope he hasn't done anything to harm her. I'm a bit surprised she hasn't tried to get away from him."

"Me, too. But I'd guess she was probably afraid to attempt anything at first. They've been gone from their house for a week now, though. If she was with him all that time, she must have seen some of the things he's done. Like break into our office."

I pushed my mug of cappuccino aside to let it cool a bit. "There's another possibility we haven't considered."

"What's that?"

"Drugs."

"I remember you talked about a methamphetamine lab over in Antioch."

"Not that kind of drugs, babe. Knockout pills, or even injected drugs like they used on you in Israel." Her captors had kept her sedated during most of that ordeal.

Jill's eyes clouded. "Oh, God, I don't even want to think about that. But you're right. Molly could be in that motel room now, while Chad is out roaming around."

The horrifying memory of Jill's captivity spooked her so badly she flinched when the phone rang. I grabbed it and answered.

"Tune said he'd head out toward Smyrna shortly," Phil Adamson said. "I told him we'd meet at the motel office in half an hour."

"Good. We were just talking about the possibility that Molly could be in the motel room now, sedated with drugs."

"We'll see. By the way, I called the deputy in Murfreesboro who's a student in my class and asked him about Tune. He says the guy is one of the bright lights in the sheriff's office down there."

I DROVE WITH A BIT MORE RATIONALITY THIS TIME. The Metro Police chief had been on a crusade lately to slow down

Nashville's speedy motorists, and I didn't want to get delayed by a motivated cop. Schools were letting out, also, making it necessary to ease through a couple of school zones. We arrived at the Old Country Inn a little after three and found Phil's white Malibu parked in front. A Rutherford County Sheriff's car pulled in as we headed for the door.

Phil met us just inside the office. "We're a little too late," he said. "They're gone."

Jill exhaled a low sigh.

"How long?" I asked.

"Less than an hour ago." He turned to the stocky black man behind us dressed in a white shirt, tie, and blue windbreaker. "Kevin Tune?"

Tune smiled and stuck out his hand. "You must be Detective Adamson. And these are the McKenzies?"

I shook hands and introduced Jill.

"I've never worked with any private eyes," Tune said. He looked back at Phil. "Did I hear right that this Rowe guy split?"

"Yeah. Come on in. I just started questioning the clerk."

We gathered around the front desk, where the same tall blonde we had talked to earlier waited solemnly. Phil introduced the new players and asked her to repeat what she had just told him.

"Mr. Casey, or whatever his name is, came in here about an hour ago and said he wanted to check out. He paid his bill in cash and left in his truck. His wife didn't come in, but I could see somebody in the passenger seat of the truck."

"Was this the big black Dodge Ram?" I asked.

"Yes, sir."

"Did you see anything of a red Nissan Sentra?"

"That's the wife's car. He said they'd come back for it later. When he was here a week ago, I told him it would be all right to leave the car till they returned. I'm sure they'll come back for it."

A week ago? That meant they had stayed here after moving out of the house in Antioch. As for Chad's coming back after Molly's car, I wasn't quite so sure. Apparently, Phil wasn't either.

"I wouldn't trust this guy to read the label on a can of beans," Phil said.

I turned to him. "That black Dodge was here when our house was broken into. He had some other means of transportation to Hermitage and back."

"Or else it wasn't him."

"It had to be him, Phil. No one else had a reason to leave that message."

"Then somebody brought him back or he's got another vehicle hidden around here."

"There are lots of little back roads in this area," Tune said. "I worked around here when I was on patrol."

Phil looked back to the clerk. "Did this Casey guy say anything else to you?"

"He wanted to know if anybody had asked about him."

"What did you say?" I asked.

She hesitated. "I told him about you and your wife. You didn't tell me not to." She looked on the verge of tears.

Jill smiled at her. "That's okay. Don't worry about it."

But Phil gave me a wary look. "Not good."

I had to agree. Chad knew we definitely had not butted out. We were hot on his trail and getting closer. Bashing in the door and spray painting a wall were signs of anger. What would he do next?

Phil turned to Tune. "Let's go check the room and see if he left anything that'd be of help."

The deputy got a key from the clerk, and we trooped around to the rear of the motel. The muggy air had the freshly washed smell that followed a spring rain. And even though the rain had ended, the asphalt of the parking lot still had a smooth sheen to it. Molly's car remained where we had seen it earlier. Tune unlocked the door to room 117 and we went inside.

"Shouldn't we be careful of what we touch?" Jill asked. She had moved into her CSI mode.

"Good idea," Tune said. "But this isn't a crime scene. We're just looking for something that might give us a hint Rowe was involved in a murder, or anything that could give us an idea where he went."

Phil dumped the contents of a wastebasket on the floor and began probing it with a pencil. "Don't see any blood traces, nothing that might show somebody was involved in a bloody confrontation."

"Don't you think he would have done away with any clothing that might have gotten bloody?" I said. "The guy seems to be pretty adept at covering up his trail. I'm convinced he burned down the house he moved out of so nobody could tell what he'd been up to, probably making meth. We also found our office broken into on Sunday, with nothing missing but the file on Molly's case. I know it was him, but he didn't leave a trace."

I briefed the two investigators on what we had learned about the man who was a former Green Beret, a Gallatin native with a record for bank robbery.

"You've been busy this past week," Phil said. "Wish I could get that kind of dedication out of a couple of guys that work with me." He gave me a broad grin. "Would you like to help out with the Bernstein case?"

"Ha," Jill said. "I heard Greg tell a friend Metro wouldn't even ask his help on a drunk and disorderly case."

Phil stuck his hands up. "Don't get your shorts in such a knot, pal. Things aren't all that bad now. About the only ones that still hold a grudge are those close to Tremaine, including some of the patrol guys who work with his brother-in-law."

I hoped he was right.

After combing through the small amount of trash in the wastebaskets, checking chairs, the desk, the bedding, the detectives agreed they had found nothing of significance. Noting a couple of plastic cups on the bathroom sink that had been stripped of their covers, I suggested Phil take them along to check for fingerprints.

"That would nail our ID of Chad Rowe."

He agreed and bagged the cups.

We headed out to the red Sentra and gazed through the windows. Nothing appeared to have been moved.

Tune absently fiddled with his tie. "I'll get a search warrant and check the car, see if there might be any bloody clothes or a knife in there. I questioned everyone around the area where the body was found, but nobody saw anything."

Both officers said they would put out bulletins in their counties in an effort to locate Chad's black Dodge pickup. I gave them the license number and agreed that seemed to be the best we could do at the moment. When we got back to our cars in front of the motel, I thanked Kevin Tune for his help and promised to let him know if I learned anything regarding Chad's whereabouts.

Phil opened the door to his car and paused for a moment. "Sorry we were a bit late getting here, Greg. Evidently he came right back out here after breaking into your house."

"Yeah. And I keep wondering if we passed him on the way home. I had no way of knowing what kind of vehicle he was driving. And I was in such a rush everything on Bell Road seemed a blur."

"I can attest to that," Jill said. "I was hanging on for dear life."

Phil chuckled. "You'd better shape up, Greg. These wives've got our numbers. You should hear mine sometimes. I'll let you know what I find on these cups." His face sobered. "I hate that that girl told Rowe about you two. Better keep that nine handy."

I got in my Jeep and felt the heft of the Beretta in its holster. Then I sat there for a minute as the two officers drove off. Something I had seen around here didn't quite fit. Something I should have looked into. What was it?

Jill crossed her arms. "Are we just going to sit here, or are you thinking about checking into the motel so we can do our clandestine lovers' act?"

"Not a bad idea," I said. "But first I have to figure out what's bugging me. Something back there around Molly's car. Let's go have another look."

I drove to the rear of the parking lot and stopped near the Sentra.

"Looks the same as it did before," Jill said.

"True, but..." I let my gaze drift along the fence. Then I saw it. "There. Right behind where Chad's truck was parked. See the trail into the woods. Somebody has scraped mud onto the edge of the asphalt."

I got out of the car and squatted to check the glob of mud. Jill stood beside me as I found a stick and poked into it.

"This is fresh," I said. "Remember how hard it rained when we were here earlier?"

"Meaning somebody has been on that trail recently."

"Right. And most likely it was Chad Rowe. The question is why did he go back there? Was he getting rid of some bloody clothes? A knife? Or Molly?"

She gasped. "Don't even think that, Greg."

I had to consider the possibility, though I knew she didn't want to. I was even less optimistic about Molly's survival after learning what had happened to Tony Yarnell. "Chances are he went back there for some reason."

"Then hadn't we better go see?"

I looked at her shiny black pumps. "We?"

She followed my gaze. "Okay. My flats are in the Cessna and I'm not exactly dressed for a hike."

"So wait in the car while I check out the trail." I looked around. "Better drive up to the back of the motel. Look like you're waiting for your clandestine lover. Do you have your .38 and your cell phone?"

She patted her bag.

"Keep an eye out for Chad," I said. "If you see anything of him, call me immediately."

She looked back as she turned toward the Jeep. "You be careful, too, dear."

After watching her drive toward the motel, I stepped over the fence onto the trail. Weeds and tall bushes crowded both sides, shedding water like sprinklers as I brushed against them. Though my waterproof jacket took it all in stride, my black pants got the worst of it. Tall oaks, spreading maples, ash, and slick-barked sycamores grew close together, leaving little room to walk anywhere but along the path. Some of the trees had begun to leaf out, though I could see a fair distance except where pockets of haze from the high humidity hung like sheer curtains.

I moved slowly, picking my steps with care to aim for piles of leaves or flat rocks that stuck out of the mud. I kept shifting my gaze from side to side in hopes of finding something beside the trail that didn't belong. But nothing stood out other than an occasional fast food container, a rusted bucket, and a few faded fragments of old newspaper sheets.

After a hundred yards or so, the trail curved around the banks of a rushing stream that bubbled like a fountain from the recent rain. Off to the right, the charred remains of a long-dormant campfire left its black slash of a signature on the earth. Vegetation that had rotted over the winter tainted the air with an acrid smell. A few birds twittered overhead, then flew off into the haze. I wasn't sure how far I had come, but I was debating about calling it quits when a dark shape in the distance caught my attention.

I quickened my pace, sinking one foot into the squishy depths of a mud hole. That triggered a curse that would've brought a quick reprimand from Jill. As I got closer, I realized I was nearing the end of the wooded area. Shortly, I came to a toppled-down fence and the rusted remains of a metal gate. I stepped into a clearing covered with dead grass and low weeds that showed signs of new green growth. Though I could see nothing on one side because of trees and a small hill, the sounds of traffic roaring along the interstate traveled clearly through the heavy, damp air. What I saw on the other side, however, startled me. The dark shape that had first caught my attention through the trees now took on the contours of a black pickup truck. The vehicle sat just beyond what looked like a rutted old wagon trail. As I walked toward it, I realized I had stumbled onto an extended cab Ford Ranger. Footprints in the soft earth led from the truck to the path I had followed in.

I stared, my heart racing, my mind grasping at the implications. Could this be the truck I had seen yesterday on Larry Inman's street? This one also had tinted windows. Could it be the same truck the neighbors thought was involved in Pedro Rodriguez's murder? The small panel that opened in the middle of the back window would make a perfect port for aiming a high-powered sniper rifle. Was it the vehicle Chad Rowe had driven to my house this afternoon?

I ran my hand around the truck's hood. It felt warm.

Somebody had driven this vehicle in the past hour or so. I checked the doors. Locked. I saw nothing on the seat. The truck bed was empty except for a large plastic storage box. I climbed up and examined the lock and the hinges. They did not appear too substantial.

I debated what to do. My first thought was to call Phil Adamson. But he would have to get back in touch with Kevin Tune, who would need to go before a judge and get a search warrant. That could take hours. But if anything incriminating remained in this truck, how long would Chad leave it here?

The police could not open the storage box without a warrant or whatever they found would be tainted evidence. I was not the police. Chad could prosecute me for breaking and entering, but that was the least of my worries. I jumped down to the ground and looked under the truck bed. I found the spare tire but no tire tool. It was probably inside the cab.

Then I remembered the rusted gate. I navigated back through the wet grass and wrestled loose a flat piece of iron about two feet long. Returning to the truck bed, I used the iron bar to pry the hinges loose on the plastic box. Lifting the lid, I stared inside. A Russian Dragunov SVD sniper rifle with an optical sight lay in a special compartment. The Dragunov I knew. It fired a 7.62mm round. Other weapons included a 9mm semiauto pistol and an M-4 military automatic rifle. Taking out my pen camera, I shot several views of the inside of the box. Then I called Phil on my cell phone. It went immediately to his voice mail. I knew what that meant. Busy.

32

EMERGING FROM THE WOODS, I found Jill waiting behind the wheel. The look on her face resembled a brewing storm.

"Where in the world have you been, Greg? Do you realize it's nearly five o'clock?" She opened the door and shoved her feet onto the pavement.

I had been too absorbed in my find to notice the time, but I made a feeble effort to defuse the situation. "Do we have an appointment?"

"Appointment, my eye. You had me worried silly. I didn't know whether to strike out on my own after you or call for reinforcements. What have you been doing, working on your hiking merit badge?"

I opened the passenger door for her. "If you'll calm down, I'll tell you. Why didn't you call me if you were that concerned?"

"Knowing you, I figured you might be sneaking up on someone. I didn't know if your phone was set on vibrate. I was afraid my call would blow your cover."

"Good thinking, babe." I patted her shoulder and grinned as I walked around to the driver's side. "First, did you see anything of Chad?"

"All I saw was a car with a couple of men dressed like business people and one with an old man and a woman."

"Well, what I saw was a shocker. I know how Chad most likely got to our house and back."

I told her about the truck and the storage box and showed her the Virginia license number I had jotted down in my notebook.

"From the traffic sounds, I could tell the clearing is near the interstate," I said. "Chad must have scouted out the area earlier and found that old road."

"Are you going to call Phil?"

"Already tried." I flipped open the cell phone and punched in his number again, then shut it with a loud snap.

"No answer?"

"Still busy. I have another idea. I just hope Art Finley hasn't left yet."

I checked the number for Heritage Car Rentals and called. He was there.

"Greg McKenzie, Art. I have a quick question for you."

"Shoot."

"The day we first came by to see you was a week ago yesterday."

"I remember."

"Well, I have a little confession. We didn't feel we could tell you at the time, but Molly Saint was the client who hired us."

"That floozy wife of Damon's?"

"She has a problem and wanted us to check into his background. That was on Monday, the day before we talked to you. She said he had taken a car to Chattanooga that morning. Can you check your records and tell me the make and color of car he drove down there?"

"Why do you want to know that?"

"I'm just looking into an angle that might mean something, might not. Can you do it for us?"

"I'll have to dig around in the files. I can do it, of course. I suppose you need to know right now?"

"As soon as possible, Art. It's pretty important."

"Okay." The way he said it conveyed that I was becoming a pain in the posterior. "I'll check on it and call you back." I gave him my cell number.

"Why do you want to know what he was driving Monday?" Jill asked.

"Just covering all the bases. Let's wait and see what Art finds."

"Monday was the day Dr. Bernstein was shot. You're not thinking?"

"Pedro Rodriguez told the cops he saw the shooter getting into a green car, a new one."

"He also said the man he saw was black."

"I know. What Chad drove Monday may mean nothing. But that Ford Ranger I found back there matches the pickup the neighbors reported seeing after Rodriguez was killed...with a seven-point-six-two round. If Chad didn't do it, maybe he drove the shooter."

Jill reached a hand up to rub her forehead. I knew all the pressure of the afternoon was beginning to get to her. "What now?" she asked.

"I guess we head for home. You can rest while I do a little work…and wait for Phil. In all the rush of things, I neglected to make adequate repairs on that battered front door."

Jill made a noisy show of snapping her seat belt. "If that's the case, let's hope Chad hasn't paid us a return visit."

"Amen to that."

She leaned her head back against the headrest.

"Headache?" I asked.

"A little. I'll be okay."

"Close your eyes and rest."

"The way you've been driving? I might wake up dead."

I saw little danger of that at the moment. Driving north toward Nashville on I-24 presented no problems. The rush of homebound traffic clogged the southbound lanes. But Bell Road was another story as we headed east. Steady lines of vehicles fought for position in both directions. Since Jill had declined the idea of resting, I suggested she try Phil Adamson's number again. It brought the same result as before.

"He must be doing a telephone interview," Jill said. "Should we call Investigator Tune?"

"No. This is strictly Metro's business. I don't want to get Rutherford County involved without an okay from Phil."

She also checked the answering machines at home and at the office.

"Molly's boss Grant Crenshaw called both places," Jill said. She flipped the phone shut.

"Did he say what he wanted?"

"There's something strange about that man. He just asks 'have you found Molly Saint?' Not have you heard from Molly or do you know where she is? Nothing about whether or not she's okay. Maybe it's that cold, lifeless voice. It sounds almost as if he's asking have you found Molly's body."

We had reached the section where Bell Road became only one lane in either direction. I had the urge to clamp down on my horn but knew the endless line of traffic would ignore my plea to move any faster. Thinking about what Jill had just said, I realized my impression of Crenshaw had been the same. But why would he think Molly might be dead? We had told him nothing about our suspicions regarding her husband.

33

It was nearly six when we pulled into our driveway in Hermitage. Chad's blow had split the facing on the front door so it would not latch securely, but I had armed the burglar alarm. No one had set it off during our absence. I had also locked the wrought iron security door, though that hadn't deterred Chad with his lock-picking skills. I concluded that he had bashed in the door when he hadn't managed to bypass the digital keypad, or else he did it purposely to inflict damage and to announce his presence. We hurried inside and punched in the code to disable the alarm.

I turned off the cell phone and used the portable in the kitchen to try Phil's number again. This time I left him a message to call me immediately.

"Don't you think Art Finley's had time to dig up that

paperwork for a week ago Monday?" Jill asked. She stood at the counter chopping several pieces of fresh fruit for a salad.

"Yeah, if he didn't get sidetracked."

When I called him, Finley apologized. "Sorry. I looked it up, but before I could call you back, I got embroiled in a knotty problem around here. I should have left for home an hour ago."

"No sweat," I said. "I'm the one who interfered with your day. I appreciate the help."

"Okay. Let's see. Damon drove out of here around eleven o'clock that morning in a new green Dodge Intrepid."

I thanked him, dropped the phone into its cradle and turned to Jill. "A new green car."

"Didn't you tell Phil Adamson there were hundreds of new green cars in Nashville?"

"I did. But it adds one more suspicious item to the list."

"And what do you plan on doing with your list?"

I picked up the phone. "Run it by Detective Adamson."

When I got his voice mail, I left a message sure to snag his attention.

"This is Greg. I've found somebody who was driving around in a new green Dodge the morning Dr. Bernstein was shot. And today he was driving a black Ford Ranger with tinted windows and a sniper rifle. I'm not budging from here until you return my call." I knew he had our home number but I gave it to him again.

Jill put our salad bowls on the table, along with glasses of fruit tea and strawberry mini-muffins. "Let's eat," she said, "so we'll be ready for whatever the next move might be."

When we finished, I returned to the living room to check out the damaged door. Jill followed me in but said she needed to lie down, her headache had begun thumping like a drum beat.

I nodded toward the recliner. "Why don't you kick back over there? I'll work quietly."

"That's okay. I think I'll go up to the bedroom where I can get more comfortable. Call me as soon as you hear from Phil."

"Will do," I said.

Chad Rowe had done a wrecking job on the door facing. Traces of brown dirt similar to the mud we'd found behind the motel stained the outside of the door. His shoe had slammed into it with such force the dead bolt had split off a large piece of the wooden jamb and the wall trim, letting the door swing open freely. I could do a temporary patch job, but I needed to bring in a carpenter to replace the jamb with a metal-reinforced model. I didn't want to risk a repeat performance by Mr. Saint/Rowe or anybody else. I'd get the carpenter to bulk up the other doors as well.

Out in the garage, I found a piece of scrap wood in the box beside my workbench. Using my power screwdriver and a few long wood screws, I patched the gap to give the dead bolt a more secure housing. Surveying my handiwork, I had to admit the result wouldn't be too pleasing to Jill's sensitive eye.

I climbed the carpeted stairway and found her sound asleep on the bed. She was still fully dressed except for her shoes. Her handbag lay beside her. As I stood in the doorway looking at her, I thought of all the years we had spent together, now nearing forty. She was a jewel. How lucky could a guy get?

As I headed down the stairs, I checked my watch and began to feel a disturbing concern. Phil Adamson should have returned my call by now. Something didn't seem quite right. I was about to pick up the phone when the front door chimes rang.

I hurried to the door and pulled it open, half expecting to see my detective friend. Instead, I found a black deliveryman in a light blue uniform and matching cap. His truck was parked behind him, though I couldn't make out the company.

"Mr. McKenzie?" he asked in an odd, high-pitched voice.

"That's me. What do you have?"

"A package. You need to sign for it." His drawl was so thick he might've had a mouthful of mush.

He held a box, about ten inches square. I couldn't recall anything I had ordered. I was a bit leery of strange packages, but I would check it out closely before opening it.

I pushed open the security door and reached for the box. Instead, he slid the package under one arm and handed me a pen and a pad he pulled from a large patch pocket.

"Just sign that," he said. "I'll put this on the table."

He stepped inside and set the box on an end table as I glanced at the receipt pad. It had my name and address and beneath that "one box." No further explanation. I noticed a brown smudge on the paper. As I looked up I found myself staring into the dark barrel of a 9mm semiautomatic pistol.

"Close the door," he said. It was not a request. And it was not the same high-pitched voice.

I pushed the door shut with my foot while closely checking his face and the hand holding the gun. Under the living room light, the brown of his face and hand had an oily sheen. I thought of the smudge on the pad. It all came together in a searing flash. The black Opryworld assassin was pure illusion.

"Chad?" I said.

34

"Get your wife in here, McKenzie," he ordered.

Now I had no doubt. The voice was that of Chad Rowe. The message sent a cold chill down my spine. I damned sure did not want Jill involved in this encounter. I can be a pretty convincing liar, and I put on a world-class performance. "She's gone shopping," I said. "She and Wilma Gannon go every Wednesday night."

"If you're lying, you're both dead."

I prayed she was still sleeping soundly and would not come wandering down the stairs. "What do you want?"

"I want you out of my way, McKenzie. You've been meddling in things you should have left alone."

"I only did what Molly hired me to do."

"Damn Molly. She's pressed her luck too far as well."

His demeanor was calm, cool, deliberate. No twitch in his face, no tremble in his hand. He held the pistol with a relaxed familiarity. The dark eyes Molly had described as looking into her soul appeared hard as agate. As I watched him, the whole scenario rolled out in my mind like pictures in a tapestry. The black assassin on the surveillance tapes appeared no blacker than this painted face. The mirror in his basement "workshop" in Antioch and the tall wooden cabinet with hooks made a perfect setup for working on disguises. I thought of the phone number for the Gold Curtain Dinner Theatre, where he had likely inquired about costumes or theatrical makeup.

Chad's low, resonant voice jarred me out of my speculations. "How did you track us down to the motel?"

"One of your driver friends told Art Finley you had talked about the Old Country Inn. Art passed the word on to me. Where's Molly now?"

"She's where she won't cause any damn problems until I decide how to take care of her." His face relaxed into a slight grin. "Funny thing, I was beginning to sort of like the old bitch. I married her because it provided a good cover, but she didn't turn out too bad. Excellent cook, good lay, used to mind her own business. Then she got too demanding. Kept bugging me to take her to some damned concert or other. I've had enough on my mind lately, didn't need any of that shit. I told her to get lost. Now her nosiness has got her into big trouble with somebody else."

I debated how to handle him. He was a pro with guns and ex-Special Forces. Any attempt to disarm him would be suicide. I could keep him talking, but what would the delay achieve? It would only increase the likelihood of Jill wandering into his line of fire. Phil Adamson should have called long before now. If he did, would Damon let me talk? How could I convey the message that I was in trouble and needed help?

"Molly mentioned you had jumped onto her about the concert business," I said, my voice conciliatory. "That was one of the things that disturbed her. It made her afraid. Somebody at the office had told her about Vietnam vets who did destructive things. I told her that was mostly a lot of crap. But she said she'd seen you chase a neighbor's dog with a machete. That really shook her up."

"Ah, shit." He grimaced. "I shoulda known it was something like that. Damn woman has too big an imagination."

"Why don't you take her out for a nice dinner?" I said. Then, thinking of the workshop story, I added, "Give her another ring you made. Women like that sort of thing. Make up to her and put all this behind you."

"It's too late for that," he said. He looked around and waved the gun toward the sofa. "Sit. I know you're an ex-Air Force cop. Don't get any bright ideas."

Right now I was fresh out of ideas. I walked over to the sofa and did as he instructed.

"What have you told the cops about me?" He moved to a chair across from me. The gun barrel faced me as an ominous black circle aimed dead center of my forehead.

I gave him a puzzled look. "Why would I tell the cops anything about you?"

"Don't play dumb. I know you've been talking to Detective Adamson. I know about your trips to Indianapolis and St. Louis. You've been digging up a lot of dirt."

I recalled the notes I had dropped in Molly's file about my call to Ray Orman, but we hadn't been to St. Louis when Chad broke into the office and stole the file. "How do you know we went to St. Louis?"

"I called Ray. The sorry ass apologized for telling you about Chad Rowe."

"Do you deny being Chad Rowe?"

He wiped the back of his free hand across the uniform, leaving a brown smudge. "I don't have to deny or confirm anything for you, McKenzie. What have you told the cops?"

I knew I had to tell him something, but I didn't want to say anything that would link him to the Opryworld murder.

"At first I asked Phil if he could help me out with the investigation Molly hired us for. He couldn't because he was too tied up with the Bernstein shooting. When he asked later how the investigation was going, I told him we didn't seem to be getting anywhere."

"You didn't tell him about Chad Rowe?"

"No. Why should I?"

"Anybody ask you about the house fire?"

I folded my arms and noticed my palms getting sweaty. I had a hunch time was running out. "Nobody but your landlord."

"You hear any more from this Tony Yarnell?"

Tony's name had been in the file also. "I heard his body was found this morning down near Smyrna."

That brought another grin. "The bastard was after Molly. I'd already been hired to take care of her."

I wasn't sure what he meant by that, but before I could

make another comment, the outside floods flashed on, signaling another visitor. Facing the window, I caught it immediately.

Chad saw the reflection on the wall and jumped up, still pointing the pistol at me.

"Somebody must have driven up," he said. "Probably your wife. Go see who it is." He had replaced the melodious tone with one of pure venom. "Don't open the damn door till I tell you, and don't try any tricks or it'll be your last."

I walked to the door, careful to keep my hands away from my body. With my eye at the peephole, I saw Phil Adamson getting out of his white Malibu.

35

I TURNED TO CHAD. "It's Adamson. He was supposed to call me."

"I cut the phone line."

That figured. And I had turned off the cell phone as usual when we got home.

"He'll know somebody's here," I said.

"When he knocks, open the door and invite him in. Close the door behind him and don't move."

The normally cheerful door chimes seemed to sound a melancholy note. He rang three times as I hesitated, but I saw no alternative to obeying Chad's orders. I opened the door and looked out at Phil, my face a blank. Chad was out of his line of sight. I knew if the detective came in with his weapon drawn, Chad would open fire.

"Come on in, Phil," I said, pushing the security door open.

As soon as he stepped inside, he spotted the black deliveryman with the pistol and froze.

Chad pointed beyond the sofa. "Both of you move very slowly and lean your palms against the wall. You know the drill."

He patted Phil down and relieved him of his .40 caliber Glock 22. Then he did the same to me, though I had already left my Beretta on my desk in the den. When Chad told us to turn around, Phil frowned at me.

"What the hell's going on, Greg?"

"Meet Chad Rowe, alias Damon Saint," I said.

Chad held the gun with both hands. Tension cranked up. "McKenzie claimed he hadn't told you anything about me. The bastard's lying, of course."

Chad had pocketed Phil's semiautomatic, and he stood back even with the foyer, too far away for us to have any chance of jumping him.

Phil turned his head toward me. "I tried to return your call, but your phone is out of order and I only got voice mail on the cell."

"Thanks to Mr. Rowe."

"What were you going to tell him, McKenzie?" Rowe asked.

I decided to see if I might rattle him. Maybe it would give us a chance to do something. I decided if either Phil or I survived, the one left should know the truth.

"Detective Adamson and I and an investigator for

Rutherford County checked out the motel shortly after you left this afternoon," I said. "They're looking at you as a suspect in the stabbing of Tony Yarnell."

"So what." Chad sneered. "What if I told you it was self-defense?"

"People defending themselves don't normally throw the assailant off a bridge," Phil said.

"After they left," I continued, "I noticed a trail back into the woods behind where your truck had been parked. I followed it all the way back to a clearing. I found a black extended cab Ford Ranger parked there. When I opened the storage box in the back, I found an assortment of weapons, including a Dragunov rifle with a sniper scope."

Phil stared at Chad. "You shot the Mexican kid on Hillandale Street?"

Chad glared at me. "Very smart, McKenzie."

"I also had Art Finley look up the records of the car you drove to Chattanooga the day Dr. Bernstein was shot. He said it was a new green Dodge Intrepid, the car Pedro Rodriguez saw in the hotel parking lot. What did you do with the .22 rifle you used on the Chairman?"

"I've heard enough of this shit, gentlemen. It's time to say good night and get the hell out of here. I have six rounds available, and as you know from my Opryworld performance, I only require one shot each."

While we talked, I had planned my final move. I knew Phil had been doing the same. I stood beside the sofa, where one of Jill's fancy cushions was in easy reach. I would scoop it up with a sweep of my arm and throw it toward Chad's gun hand. He would likely get off one shot, but my hope was the cushion would delay him long enough for Phil to nail him. If I were lucky, I would take a non-fatal hit. I tried not to think of the alternative.

As I saw Chad aim the gun toward Phil, I started swinging my arm. He caught the movement immediately, yelled, "Die, dammit!" and shifted the weapon in my direction. As I scooped up the cushion, the shot rang out. I didn't feel it, but I knew I was a dead man.

36

I NEEDED ONLY AN INSTANT to realize the shot sounded more like the pop of a .38 than the crack of a 9mm. I had blinked my eyes shut, and as I opened them I saw Chad crumple to the floor. More nimble than me, Phil was on top of him in an instant, reaching for the gun. I heard another sound like a body falling and moved past the two men to find Jill slumped against the stair railing about halfway down from the landing. She still clutched her small .38 revolver.

My heart was pumping in overdrive as I knelt beside her on the stairway. "Babe, are you all right?"

She had a glazed look in her eyes as I took the gun from her hand. "Is he…?" Her voice trailed off as she tried to speak.

I knew what she was asking. I turned to look back in the living room and saw Phil talking into his cell phone. "I don't know," I said.

Phil walked over to the bottom of the stairs. "Are you okay, Mrs. McKenzie?" At the distraught look on her face, he came up to kneel beside me. "If that round had hit anywhere else, you'd be a widow now. It apparently struck his spinal cord at the base of the skull, paralyzing him instantly so he couldn't squeeze the trigger."

He looked around at me. "I need to thank you both for saving my hide. That was a brave thing you did, tossing the pillow to distract him."

"I don't know if it was brave or foolish," I said. "But I couldn't just stand there and let him have his way."

I handed Phil the .38, then sat beside Jill and held her in my arms. Her body shook with sobs. She had saved my life, but I knew she'd pay a price for it. A woman who detested violence and despised guns for many years, she would have a tough time coming to grips with what she had done, even though she knew she had no choice. I hated the necessity of taking a life as well, but I was eternally grateful she'd had the guts to pull that trigger.

"Paramedics are on the way," Phil said, "but I think it's a job for the ME. Stormy's also en route."

Captain Stormy Weathers was head of the Homicide Division. He had taken offense at the newspaper story that caused all my problems with the department. However, he later passed on word through Phil that he knew things were taken out of context, and he realized I had my reasons for the views I held regarding Detective Tremaine.

I looked at Phil. "Let me borrow your phone a moment."

I used it to call Wilma Gannon and asked her to come over to be with Jill. I knew I would be busy for the next hour or so dealing with homicide officers.

When the ambulance arrived, I tried to get Jill up to the bedroom, but she insisted on remaining glued to her spot on the stairs. She had quit sobbing and was calmed down enough to get her thought processes going again.

"The doorbell chiming woke me up," she said in a low voice. "I wondered who it could be. When I got to the top of the stairs, I heard an angry voice. Then I saw that horrid man with the gun. I hurried back to the bedroom for my pistol, then came down the stairs far enough to get a good look at him. When he pointed his gun and said something about one shot each, I knew what I had to do. I was already aiming. When he yelled, 'Die,' I fired."

"Thank God you did it," I said.

She stared down at her hands for a moment, then back up at me. "Where do you suppose Molly is? Do you think she's all right?"

"He has her stashed away somewhere," I said. "We'll find her."

I headed into the living room as a Metro Fire Department paramedic squatted beside Chad. I told Phil about Jill's concerns, that we needed to find Molly.

After the paramedic checked Chad's vital signs, he shook his head.

"He's beyond us."

I stared at the carpet. The wound had resulted in massive bleeding. A large red pool had soaked into the carpet. I'd have to get somebody out to replace it as soon as possible. I would cover the red stain with a small throw after they removed the body so Jill wouldn't have to look at it.

Captain Weathers came in just after the ambulance crew. He was a big man with short black hair and the ready frown of a cop who had seen too much. His dark green tie was pulled askew beneath a brown checked jacket. He looked at Phil, then glanced my way.

"So you think this is the guy who shot Bernstein?"

"He admitted it," I said.

"In so many words," Phil added. "When he was about to shoot Greg and me, he said after his Opryworld performance we should know he only needed one shot for each of us."

The captain leaned over to look at the body. "Damn. He painted himself black." He straightened up and turned to me. "Your wife took him out?"

I nodded as Phil pulled the .38 out of his pocket and showed it to Weathers. "All three of us have handled it, but that shouldn't be a problem. The facts are clear. I have Rowe's nine in an evidence bag."

"Jill is still sitting up on the stairs where she was when she fired the shot," I said, pointing toward her.

Weathers looked up at her. "Hello, Mrs. McKenzie. We'll need to talk to you, but that can wait."

By then two uniforms had come in, and when I turned toward the door, there stood Mark Tremaine, looking quite solemn and useless, along with another homicide detective. They moved over to let a couple of FBI agents and a Secret Service man slide past them. An associate from the medical examiner's office walked in afterward.

"Damn, guys, this ain't Grand Central Station," Captain Weathers growled. "You got another room we can use until the ME is finished, McKenzie?"

I led them to the dining room that opened off the kitchen, where we had a table that seated ten. After several of the players got off into the corners, their backs turned to use their cell phones, the whole entourage joined me around the table. Phil and I took turns outlining what had happened tonight and the events that led up to it. When I was questioned about the phone number that took us to St. Louis, I said truthfully that I had found it at the house Chad and Molly had vacated. I didn't bother to mention the place had been burned down first.

Captain Weathers and his detectives kept the discussion offbeat with dark comments like "old Saint sure resembled Shad Roe with his marbles spilled on the floor." It was a macabre brand of humor homicide guys used in an attempt to keep their gruesome job from overpowering them.

We were interrupted a couple of times by the captain's cell phone. One call advised that the delivery truck parked out front had been stolen during the afternoon. Later he was told that Chad's Dodge Ram had been found in a parking lot not far from where he had stolen the truck.

By the time we finished, the Metro crew seemed pleased the case was over and ready for the file books. The FBI and Secret Service guys showed no such pleasure. Their job was just starting. They faced the task of tracking down who had sent Chad Rowe to kill Dr. Bernstein.

I was instructed to bring Jill downtown to the Criminal

Justice Center in the morning for our official statements. Before we adjourned, I brought up my major concern.

"We need to find my client, Molly Saint," I said. "I have a hunch he's got her drugged or tied up in a motel somewhere around here."

"I've already dispatched some guys to Rutherford County to get that black Ford Ranger," Weatherly said. "The crime scene techs are examining everything in Rowe's Dodge Ram. Hopefully they'll find something that'll lead us to her."

After the cops cleared out, I sat in the kitchen and talked with Jill and Sam and Wilma Gannon.

"How're you making it, babe?" I asked, holding her hand across the table.

She smiled, a good sign. "Better. Wilma and Sam have done a lot of talking. I'll have to say after what happened to Tim back in October, they know how to handle emotionally charged issues."

Their son Tim was the victim in the murder case Jill and I had solved down in Florida a few months ago. They were a perfect example of what friendship was all about.

I had just jumped into the conversation when the phone rang. I answered the wall phone beside the counter. "This is Greg."

"Grant Crenshaw, Mr. McKenzie. I understand the police determined that Damon Saint, Molly's husband, was the one who killed Chairman Bernstein."

"Where did you hear that?" I asked.

"It was on the TV news a few minutes ago. Have you found Molly?"

There it was again, that cold, unemotional question, as if she were no more than a bag of clothes. "No, but the police are searching for her. We think Damon may have left her bound and gagged in a motel. Maybe drugged."

"I see. Do you have any idea which motel?"

What was with this guy? If we had any idea, we would already have rescued her.

"No, Mr. Crenshaw," I said. I looked around at Jill and shook my head.

"Very well, Mr. McKenzie. I'll see what I can find out elsewhere."

You do that, I thought. And quit annoying me.

37

Phil Adamson called early the next morning with word they had located Molly. The clerk at a sleazy motel on the southeastern side of the city saw TV coverage of the story and thought he recognized Chad's black pickup truck. When he heard the wife might have been drugged and left in a motel, he recalled watching the pickup driver lead a woman who appeared drunk into the room. He called the cops.

Molly was in a groggy, drug-induced haze when they found her. An ambulance had transported her to the hospital, where the doctors said it would be a few hours before she could answer questions coherently.

"Since she obviously trusts you guys," Phil said, "I think it might be useful for you to be on hand when she comes around."

We met Phil and a nerdy-looking FBI agent named Markovich around nine in a crowded hospital waiting room with abstract prints on the wall. I thought I recognized one as a weird Salvador Dali painting that showed a watch bent in the middle and hanging off a table like it was made of melted wax. A family ranging from white-haired grandparents to teens in baggy pants that barely clung to their hips huddled in one corner, the grownups talking in subdued voices. We moved to the other side of the room.

"They say she'll be ready to talk to us in a few minutes," Phil said.

Agent Markovich, who might have been fresh out of college but for the thinning hair in front, eyed me with a quirky grin. "Aren't you the guy who got my boss all riled up a while back when you were with the DA's office?"

Jill nudged my arm. "It's confession time, Greg."

"Guilty," I said.

Phil laughed, something I'd seldom heard him do. "Greg has a knack for getting people riled up. But he usually knows what he's doing, like with this case."

"I knew some McKenzies when I was growing up in Chicago," Markovich said. "The old man wore his kilt on ceremonial occasions. Us kids used to laugh about the skirt, but my dad warned me those old Scots could be pretty ferocious."

"That's true," I said. "My granddaddy fought with a Highland regiment in the First World War."

Markovich squinted his eyes. "Did they go into battle dressed like that?"

"They sure did. My dad told me about a German he met

right after World War II who'd been a junior officer in the Nazi 1st SS Panzer Division. The guy claimed the Waffen SS were by far the toughest soldiers around. But he admitted they were afraid of the Scottish Highlanders. They called them 'Devil Soldiers Wearing Skirts.'"

"No kidding?" Markovich chuckled.

"It's true. This guy said he was in one encounter between a dismounted 1st SS Panzer unit and the Highlanders. He said the first warning they had was when they barely heard bagpipes in the distance. There had been a lot of rumors about what the Highlanders would do if they ever got their hands on a German. As they listened, the sounds of the pipers kept coming closer and closer. They were playing 'Scotland the Brave.' It spooked the Nazis so much many of them dropped their weapons and ran. He said it was the only time he'd ever seen or heard of an elite Waffen SS unit breaking and running en masse."

"Hey," Phil said, "don't you know it's a very bad idea to piss off a big, red-headed guy wearing a skirt?"

He looked around at Jill and was probably about to apologize, but she was already laughing. At any rate, the conversation ended as a nurse in a flowery smock came out to tell us Molly was ready. We followed her down a brightly lit corridor with an antiseptic smell to a corner room where Molly's bed had been cranked up to a sitting position. She looked pale and haggard, but her mouth turned up in a weak smile when she saw Jill and me.

"Mr. and Mrs. McKenzie, I didn't expect you."

Jill walked over and patted her puffy hand. An IV tube ran down to her wrist.

"We've been looking for you for a week, Molly," Jill said. "And it's Greg and Jill, not Mr. and Mrs. McKenzie. I know you're Darlene's daughter. Why didn't you tell us?"

She hung her head. "I was afraid of what you might have heard about me in the past."

"Never mind the past," Jill said. "This is Detective Adamson and Agent Markovich, Molly. They have some questions for you."

The nurse had brought in a couple of extra chairs, and we all sat around the bed. Phil led off with a question that made Jill cringe. I reached over and took her hand.

"Are you aware of what happened to your husband last night, Mrs. Saint?"

Molly exhaled a sigh. "I heard he was shot when he tried to kill you and Mr. McK...uh, Greg. I didn't know what he had done, but I suspected it was something terrible." She looked around at Jill and me. "When I went down to his workshop that morning I called you, I found a box packed with guns and knives. He had different kinds of clothes on hangers and wigs and false whiskers in a box."

Phil leaned forward in his chair. "Did you ask him about it?"

"No. I was afraid to. But when he found out I had gone down there, he demanded to know what I was doing. I said I was just looking around and was frightened by what I saw. He told me it involved a hobby but wouldn't say anything else. Then he said we were moving, that he had won a lot of money gambling and was to pick it up on Saturday. We were leaving Nashville and would buy a nice house where we were going. I didn't know what to believe."

Putting the story together from what she could recall between obvious bouts with drugs, some fed to her in drinks, Molly told of spending Wednesday night in the motel. They left her car there and drove Chad's truck to the farm in Gallatin, which he claimed belonged to a friend. She wasn't aware he had returned to Antioch that night to set the house afire, but she remembered feeling strangely groggy the next morning.

She considered making an attempt to get away, but knew Chad was always armed and feared he wouldn't hesitate to use the gun on her. Saturday afternoon, he told her the gambling debt was being paid by a man who would leave a pickup truck for him in the Gallatin Wal-Mart parking lot. He had her claim an envelope containing the key at the store's Customer Service counter. The envelope was marked "Edgar." Then she drove the Ford Ranger to the farm with Chad following her.

Until they got back to the farm, he had acted cool but considerate. Once in the house, though, he burst into a tirade. He had gone through her handbag and found our McKenzie Investigations business card. After he threatened to beat her if she didn't come clean, she confessed what she had done. That's when Chad drove to a pay phone and called to threaten me if I didn't drop the investigation.

He apparently drugged her again that night and drove to Hermitage, where he burglarized our office. On Sunday he bought a newspaper, gave part of it to Molly but kept the main news section for himself. She didn't think about it at the time, but realized now Chad was likely keeping up with the Bernstein murder case. That afternoon he told her it was time to move on, they would leave the next morning.

So far he hadn't harmed her. She decided to go along with him and watch for an opportunity to escape. She didn't believe his tale about having won the money gambling, figuring it was more likely loot from a robbery. He stashed the cash in several cardboard boxes beneath a tarpaulin in the back of the pickup. She never saw it so had no idea how much money was involved.

Monday they returned to the motel near Smyrna and got a room in back, where she had left her car parked against the fence. Molly drove the Ford Ranger, noting that now it had tinted vinyl sheets covering the windows. Chad followed closely in the Dodge. That afternoon, a strange thing happened. When Chad went out to get his shaving gear from his truck, he saw an old Chevy sitting in the parking lot with a lone black man inside. The man seemed to be watching him. Chad told Molly to go out to her car and see what would happen. When she did, the man got out of his car and started toward her. That brought Chad out of the motel. The man saw him and took off at a run, jumped into his car and sped away.

Molly told Chad she had never seen the man before, but she didn't know if he believed her.

"Must have been Tony Yarnell," Phil said. "He drove an old Chevrolet."

I agreed.

Apparently Chad guessed that Molly was getting ideas about fleeing. After that her memory turned fuzzy as a misty haze. She recalled nothing concrete until a policewoman roused her in the motel early that morning.

When Molly had finished, Agent Markovich spoke up.

"Let's go over the money again, Mrs. Saint. Did you see what he did with the boxes?"

"No. I guess he left them in the back of the truck."

"The Ford Ranger?"

"Yes."

"When I found it," I said, "there was nothing in the bed but the plastic storage box holding the weapons."

"There was no money in the Dodge Ram or the Sentra, either," Phil said.

Markovich planted his fists on his hips. "Damn. He's been roaming all over town. He could have stashed it anywhere."

"What about the farm?" Jill asked.

That triggered a picture in my mind, a dirty shovel leaning against the wall at the back of the farmhouse.

"I think you might've hit on the answer, babe," I said. "I saw a shovel behind the house at that farm. It looked like it had been used recently."

Phil and Markovich gave me skeptical looks.

"Remember my telling you about the bank robbery he was convicted of in Missouri?"

"Yeah," Phil said. "What's that got to do with it?"

"He and his partner bought a shovel and buried the loot in a cemetery. The partner dug it up while our man was in prison. Remember, this guy's real name is Chad Rowe. The partner was Damon Saint. He didn't bother to tell Rowe about the money. I'm pretty sure Rowe killed him before taking over his identity."

"Where's the farm?" Markovich asked. "If we have to,

we'll dig up the whole damned place."

I gave him directions.

"Has the little pickup given you any leads on the source of the money?" Jill asked.

"We're working on it," he said.

When we left the hospital, Molly remained in a daze over what she had just learned about her husband. Jill and I drove to the Criminal Justice Center downtown, where we were to meet with Phil and Captain Weathers. I hoped for Jill's sake it would not be a rigorous interrogation.

38

NORMALLY A CALM, DELIBERATE PERSON, Jill found it difficult to sit still as she waited to give her statement. I held her hand and assured her there would be no problem, she should simply tell them everything exactly as it happened. They interviewed us separately, which was normal. Afterward, while Jill had gone to the restroom, Phil told me she did fine, though she nearly broke down when it came to the point where she pulled the trigger.

We sat in the Homicide office with its rows of shelves filled with case files and small desk cubicles. Each detective had a laptop computer connected to the network that contained all of the photos, reports, and evidence for every case. When Jill came back, Phil smiled at her.

"Don't worry about anything," he said. "We're recommending to the DA that the case be closed. Now the Bureau boys can start earning their pay. They're probably working like mad checking all the call logs for Rowe's phone."

"They won't find anything," I said. "He was too smart to make any calls from there. The more I think about it, the more I'm inclined to buy into that story Perry Vanatta told us."

"About the clandestine government mission?" Jill asked.

"Right. He wouldn't have called his old lawyer buddy from high school without a good reason. I'd guess the CIA may have hired him for some black operation. They might even have provided additional training."

Phil's face clouded up. "Don't tell me you think this Bernstein thing was a CIA plot."

"I didn't mean it that way. I think he's probably been free-lancing as a hit man the past few years. Remember, he told us he married Molly for cover. Most of those guys are loners. His trips to help out an old Vietnam buddy could have been junkets to commit contract killings."

Phil pushed a large black binder aside and leaned an elbow on his desk. "I'll agree he really acted like a pro on this case."

I thought about a couple of things Chad had mentioned to me. In the excitement of the moment, they hadn't meant anything. Now they began to form the outlines of a picture.

"Before you came in last night, Phil, he told me Molly's nosiness had gotten her into big trouble with somebody else. Then when we were talking about Tony Yarnell being out to get her, he said something like I've already been hired to take care of her."

Jill gasped. "Do you think he planned to kill her?"

"That was the implication. As if somebody thought she

knew too much and wanted her eliminated."

"I'm afraid you've lost me," Phil said. "Knew too much about what, the Bernstein assassination?"

"I don't know. I'm sure whoever ordered the killing wouldn't have known Damon was the person hired for the job. It would have been handled through a third party who collected the money and then paid off Chad."

"Why don't we talk to Molly and ask her what she might have known that could upset someone enough to want her killed?" Jill asked.

"Wouldn't hurt," I said. "Want to go along, Phil?"

He picked up the black binder. "Thanks, but I need to get everything put in this case file. If you find anything I can follow up on, let me know."

MOLLY LOOKED LIKE A DIFFERENT PERSON when we got back to her hospital room. She had put on some makeup and was almost finished with her lunch. The smile she gave us was brighter then any I'd seen before.

"What brings you folks back?" she asked.

"I'm still troubled by some loose ends in this case," I said. "From comments Chad made to me last night, I got the impression he thought you knew something about someone that would have worried them enough to want you out of the way."

She put her fork down and folded her arms. "Out of the way? You mean, like killed?"

"That's right. Think about it, Molly. Have you been anywhere lately or done anything that gave you insight into someone's dirty deeds?"

"That's pretty wild. I haven't been anywhere lately but home or at work. I certainly didn't hear about any dirty deeds at work."

Jill and I looked at each other. I'm sure she had the same thought I did, about Grant Crenshaw's odd calls inquiring if we had located Molly.

"How close are you to Mr. Crenshaw?" I asked.

She grinned. "As close as the next office. He has a secretary, and I'm the next office over. But that's not what you mean, is it?"

"Not quite."

"As his administrative assistant, I work with him on most of his projects. He makes a lot of money and he spends a lot of money. I can't talk about anything specific. He's a stickler for confidentiality."

Jill leaned against the counter beside the bed. "Has he had any problems lately?"

"You can't run an operation like that without having problems. He's good at staying on top of things, putting out fires. I think he gets a lot of ideas from a group he belongs to. It's made up of guys like him. I think they meet sort of informally."

"A local group?" I asked.

"No. They're from all over. He's pretty close-mouthed about it. I don't know who else is involved, but I know when he's been to a meeting. They've had several recently."

"But you haven't heard anything about any major problems, something that could have a disastrous effect on business?"

She stretched her fingers and looked down at them. They glistened with a new coat of nail polish. "Oh, he's been concerned for some time about rising interest rates and how they affect several big loans. But that's not something he can do anything about."

I wasn't so sure. "Has he talked about that a lot lately?"

"I know it's been weighing on his mind." She frowned. "Say, are you thinking Mr. Crenshaw might have had something to do with what Damon did or said? That's pretty far out."

Molly still called him Damon, having yet to reconcile the fact she had been married to a man named Chad Rowe.

"You may be right," I said. "But I can't imagine anywhere else you could have learned something that would be so disturbing."

"But I don't know anything."

Jill turned to me. "What if Molly really didn't hear anything, but somebody, for some reason, thought surely she did?"

"That's a possibility," I said. "Molly, do you recall any instances where Mr. Crenshaw acted strangely around you, like he might have been suspicious? Something that made him show unusual concern?"

She was silent for a full minute, her eyes fixed on the sheet below her folded hands. Finally, she looked up. "The last day I was in the office was a Friday. I agonized over whether to ask for a few days off since I was becoming a nervous wreck about Damon. When I finally made up my mind, I started toward Mr. Crenshaw's office. The secretary had stepped out for a few minutes, and his door was closed. I was about to knock when I heard him shouting at somebody."

"Did you know who it was?" I asked.

"My door had been open and I was sure nobody had gone in Mr. Crenshaw's office. I checked the lights on the secretary's phone, but it didn't show a line in use. That meant he was using his private line that doesn't go through our phone system."

"What did you do then?"

"I walked back to his door and listened, but I didn't hear anything else. Then suddenly the door burst open and he saw me standing there. He had the strangest look on his face. It was like shock at first, then hostility. I was already stressed out. When he snapped, 'What the hell are you doing here, Molly?' I just went blank. I stammered, 'Nothing, sir,' spun around and hurried back to my office."

Jill looked down at Molly, her eyebrows pinched together. "Sounds like he thought you were eavesdropping."

"I know," she said. "But I had no idea who he was talking to or what he was saying."

Obviously, it was something he didn't want anyone to hear. "Did he bring the subject up later that day?" I asked.

"No. But when I finally went in to ask for a few days off, he was unusually curt with me. We normally get along fine. If nothing pressing was in the works, he'd say take off whatever you need. This time he wanted to know what was my problem."

"Did you tell him about Chad?" Jill asked.

"No. At that point I wasn't too sure of anything myself. I just said I had a problem that was bothering me, and I needed some time off to decide what I should do."

A disturbing picture slowly emerged as I considered all the possibilities. I had to admit it was all pure speculation, but we were talking about three days prior to the Bernstein shooting. Crenshaw had been involved with a secretive group of big money businessmen, all of whom had likely suffered the consequences of rising interest rates, thanks in no small part to the Fed chairman. The financial press recognized Dr. Bernstein as the most dominant personality to hold the job in recent memory, and he exercised tight control over the board's actions. Taking him out could have a profound effect on the Federal Reserve Board's future direction.

If Crenshaw were involved in a plot to hire a hit man to kill Bernstein, and if he believed Molly had overheard enough to implicate him in the conspiracy, he could easily have put out the word to eliminate her. And Chad would have been a logical choice to take on the job.

I was about to step out of the room to call Phil Adamson when a dark-haired man in sunglasses, his bronzed skin and athletic moves those of a tennis player, came through the door. Without the hint of a smile, he looked down at Molly, then glanced around at Jill and me. I recognized Grant Crenshaw from pictures I'd seen in the newspaper.

39

"Mr. Crenshaw," Molly said with a tentative smile. "Nice of you to come by. Meet Jill and Greg McKenzie."

"So you're McKenzie," he said, a curl to his lip. He thrust out a carefully manicured hand that I took without enthusiasm. His grip seemed powered by muscles of steel. He looked across at Jill. "I understand you're quite a shot with a .38, Mrs. McKenzie."

Jill frowned, coloring slightly. I saw a tear glisten in the corner of her eye. Even disregarding my preconceived notions about the man, I disliked him instantly.

"Happily the police finally located Molly," I said, "and she's quickly getting back to normal."

Crenshaw walked over to stand beside the bed. "I trust you'll be able to return to work soon, Molly. I have several projects that need your attention."

"Yes, sir. I hope so."

After running a hand through his tousled hair, he turned to Jill and me. "A pleasure meeting you. Now, if you'll pardon me, I have a meeting to attend." His voice had a self-exalting air to it. He looked down at Molly. "Stay well."

With that, he strode quickly from the room.

"Is he always that abrupt and aloof?" I asked Molly.

"He can be a bit difficult at times, but normally he acts very gentlemanly around me. You notice he said 'stay well.'"

What I noticed about it was the apparent insincerity. To me it sounded almost like a taunt, as if he meant just try and stay well, see what it gets you. Admittedly, I tended to think the worst of him.

I turned to Jill. "You and Molly visit a few minutes while I go out and use the cell phone."

"You can use my phone here in the room," Molly said.

"Thanks, but I think the cell phone would be a little more appropriate at the moment." I didn't want her to hear what I had to say, and I knew the digital phone would be a bit more secure.

I took an elevator down to the ground floor and walked outside the hospital entrance. Finding a quiet, secluded spot near a large redbud tree full of pinkish flowers, I punched in Phil Adamson's number. While waiting for him to pick up, I recalled the redbud was also known as the "Judas tree," which seemed appropriate for a place to report on Grant Crenshaw's activities.

"I just came across some troubling information from Molly Saint," I said when Phil answered. I quickly outlined the situation, then added, "I'm concerned about Molly's safety. Could you get a guard put on her room?"

"Captain Weathers would probably say you're moving too fast on too little hard evidence, but after the message we just received, I can probably handle him."

"What was the message?" I asked.

"The FBI just finished out in Gallatin. They dug up a cache of hundred-dollar bills that would rival a major drug bust. Around a half-mil, I understand."

That nearly floored me. "Five hundred thousand dollars?"

"Close to it. I suspect the chief won't be too eager to take on a figure like Crenshaw, though. He's pretty powerful around the Metro courthouse. Our best bet would be to turn this over to the Bureau. Let them dig into his phone calls and whatever else they can ferret out."

"Yeah. I'm well aware of the problems you can run into when tackling a high-profile businessman."

He chuckled. "I hear you."

My getting the heave as a DA's investigator stemmed from the case over which I had criticized Detective Tremaine. The missing girl was the daughter of a bank president who was the chief backer of the district attorney.

I closed the cell phone and returned to Molly's room, where Jill and I stayed until a uniformed officer arrived to guard her door.

I BRIEFED JILL ON WHAT I HAD DONE as we drove back to the office.

"Thank God you did," she said. "I worried about her after that horrid man had left. I don't think she wants to believe the worst of him, but I surely do."

I patted her hand. "He probably won't be the last to make some uncalled-for remark about what you did. You have to roll with the punches, babe. Don't let it get to you."

She was silent the rest of the way back, and I wasn't sure of what else to say.

AFTER A FEW SESSIONS WITH OUR PASTOR, Dr. Peter Trent, Jill seemed to put the trauma of that Wednesday night behind her. I knew it still lay not far beneath the surface, however. I decided to hold off for a month or so before urging her to go back to the firing range and resume target practice.

We learned through Phil Adamson that the FBI launched an immediate investigation into Grant Crenshaw and his operation. I had given them Crenshaw's private phone number, which he had left with me the first time we talked. The Bureau arranged for Molly's doctor to order a leave of absence so she could recuperate from unspecified complications of her treatment by her husband. Jill flew her out to a secluded resort in the River of No Return Wilderness Area of Idaho. After hearing about their spiraling descent between 8,000-foot mountains, I was deliriously happy I had stayed in Nashville to take care of business.

A few weeks later, they arrested Crenshaw and charged him with conspiracy to murder both the chairman of the Federal Reserve Board and Molly Saint, who had taken back her maiden name of Harrison. Crenshaw admitted his role under intense interrogation but, like Damon Saint/Chad Rowe, refused to implicate others. There were, however, several unindicted co-conspirators. Ted Kennerly learned from one of his

FBI contacts that the go-between who hired and paid Chad was believed to be a former CIA officer. The man had dealt with "outside contractors" in overseas operations where the intelligence establishment wanted someone "neutralized." They speculated that Chad had started out as one of his "contract" agents.

As usual, we wrapped up the case with one of Jill's culinary extravaganzas. Instead of a sit-down dinner this time, however, she decided to make it an indoor cookout. She spent days cleaning the house, even though it already looked great with the new paint and carpet. She strung miniature Japanese lanterns to add an outdoorsy flavor?we didn't trust the weather or the mosquitoes enough to have a truly outdoor event. We invited most of the major players, including Molly, Phil Adamson and his wife, Ted and Karen Kennerly, Art Finley, Bert Quincy, Larry Inman, and Investigator Kevin Tune from Murfreesboro. For good measure, we added Molly's brother Nick and wife Zori, plus our trusty friends Sam and Wilma Gannon.

Everyone stuffed themselves on the barbequed salmon, Swedish meatballs, chicken and shrimp kabobs, along with fresh vegetables and fruits with various dips. We wound up with a spectacular fresh strawberry, chocolate and whipped cream concoction, accompanied by coffee and drinks of choice.

When the chatter subsided a bit, Molly took the floor. She held up her wine glass. "I propose a toast to Jill and Greg. I'm sure I wouldn't be here today if it hadn't been for their dogged insistence on tracking me down. I'm happy to say I've come to terms with myself, and I learned something about family values in the process."

Drinks were gulped between calls of, "Hear, hear."

"I learned something about family, too," Jill said.

She was perched on the arm of my chair in the den, where we had set up the bar. I don't know if it was just coincidence, but everybody had mostly avoided the living room. I knew it would take Jill a good while to feel comfortable in there.

"What did you learn?" Molly asked.

"Now that we're firmly settled in Nashville, I need to do a better job of keeping in touch with what little remains of my family." She explained the relationship with Molly, for those who were not aware of it.

"And I'd like to offer a toast to this lady here," I said, putting an arm around Jill. "I definitely could not do without her."

She gave me an embarrassed smile.

"And before things get too serious," I added, "I want to thank my favorite homicide detective for coming to my rescue that fateful Wednesday evening. Phil, you couldn't have gotten here at a more opportune time."

"Thanks, old buddy," he said in a droll voice, a departure from his normal no-nonsense manner. "I also saved your rear end on another occasion. It could have put you back on the DA's you-know-what list."

"Oh? When was that?"

"When I found out you had made an unauthorized seizure of evidence in the case. A certain piece of paper bearing a phone number in St. Louis."

That caught me off guard. "What do you mean by 'unauthorized seizure'?"

"You took it from the scene of a fire under investigation, my friend."

I stared at him, rubbing my chin. "And what basis did you have to think that?"

"They found your case file among a pile of things in Rowe's truck. I assume it's one he stole from your office. Fortunately, they gave it to me." He grinned. "You're very thorough in your notes. It would've made interesting reading for Captain Weathers."

I gave him a nasty look. "What did you do with it?"

He laughed. "I should say I locked it in my safe for future leverage. Actually, I trashed it."

With that, I closed the case.

END

Praise for *Designed to Kill*
the second Greg McKenzie Mystery

"Mr. Campbell has written another page-turner...He has filled the story with such convincing characters that are so fleshed-out as to appear alive. I'm eagerly looking forward to the next...adventure. But I sincerely suggest that you don't miss this one."
Shirley Truax,
All About Murder Reviews

"Greg McKenzie...is a wonderful protagonist with an older man's wisdom, crossed with the droll voice of an unrepentant rebel...Campbell's uncluttered prose is the perfect vehicle for a mystery...a thoroughly satisfying read."
Brian Kaufman,
Roundtable Reviews

"Greg and Jill are well-written characters; their relationship is loving without being cloying and seems right for a long-married couple...The locale of the book is well described and the reader gets lots of local color as well as thrills and suspense."
Lorraine Gelly,
Reviewing the Evidence

"Campbell is a consummate writer...(he) has done it again!...He manages to hang the specter of the wrongfully murdered young architect over a plot that moves along at a rapid clip with plenty of cliffhangers and well-defined characters...A fine second effort!"
Shelley Glodowski, Senior Reviewer,
Midwest Book Review

"A thoroughly enjoyable mystery with an intelligent plot, clever clues and characters who are like people you know."
Phillip Margolin, author of nine
New York Times bestsellers

"This book seems more a logic puzzle than a mystery—until the end. That's just one of the things that makes it a sure-fire delight for anyone who likes lots of suspense and characters who are a lot like the people next door…(it) is filled with vivid and creative imagery as well as demonstrating superb writing skills."

Elizabeth K. Burton,
Blue Iris Journal

"We often hear that crime fictions are nothing more than clever escapist puzzles…what differentiates one from the other is the author's ability to provide ample plot twists that effectively sustain the narrative tension until the last chapter. Here is where *Designed to Kill* shines."

Norman Goldman,
Bookpleasures, The Best Reviews

"Mr. Campbell's wealth of life experience and military background give him an eye for detail, which is crucial in any mystery. There is a full array of colorful characters…The plotting, pace and dialog are perfect in *Designed to Kill*. This is a perfect read for the beach or a long winter afternoon.

Roberta Austin,
Murder & Mayhem Book Club

"So is *Designed to Kill* as good as *Secret of the Scroll*. Nope…it's much, much better…(when) Tim Gannon's dead body is found…the duo (Greg and Jill McKenzie) investigates, finding out some dark secrets, and shocking revelations…culminating in a…totally unexpected finish. I enjoyed the book, rather relished the work."

Narayan Radhakrishnan,
New Mystery Reader

"Greg McKenzie is an affable hero, ably abetted by his wife, Jill. It's a cleverly plotted, tightly written book."
>Sallie Bissell, author of the best-selling Mary Crow series (*In the Forest of Harm* and *A Darker Justice*)

"Everything you could want in a mystery. Suspense, colorful characters and a great surprise ending."
>Don Bruns, author of the highly acclaimed *Jamaica Blue* and *Barbados Heat*

"Greg and wife Jill look into the alleged suicide of their best friends' son in Pensacola, FL. Greg's suspicions of murder are reinforced by faulty rebar use, stolen plans, erased files, a missing key, a hot-tempered builder, a slow-to-pay developer, and a God's-gift-to-women inspector. And then two guys beat Greg up. Plenty of domestic details ground the homey narration."
>*Library Journal*

Praise for *Secret of the Scroll*
the first Greg McKenzie Mystery

Bloody Dagger Award 2nd Place Winner
ForeWord Magazine Mystery Book of the Year Finalist
Nominated for the Dorothy Parker Awards

"A superbly written book with an excellent plot. The action is on-going and riveting."
All About Murder Reviews
by Shirley Truax

"One of the finest books I have read in many years...a riveting, edge of the seat book that is set against the backdrop of the modern Middle East."
Women on Writing Reviews
by Janet Schmidt

"A thriller in every sense of the word...(Campbell sets) up cliff-hanging situations designed to keep the reader glued to his book...His writing style is as full of energy as his characters."
Midwest Book Review
by Shelley Glodowski

"A first person, narrative mystery thriller of the first order...if you like good solid writing, thoughtful characterization and a believable story you'll enjoy this book."
Rus Morgan, Host Interviewer for
PBS "Book Talk," Station WYPL,
Memphis

"Given the state of affairs in the Middle East, it's not hard to imagine a single incident igniting into a major conflict...an intriguing and entertaining thriller that shows how such a scenario might occur."
The Tennessean (Nashville)
by Stephen Doster

"This is a fast, exciting read. It grabs you and won't let you go. I couldn't put it down. I wholeheartedly recommend it."
    The Best Reviews by Judith Saul

"A fast-paced story of mystery, intrigue, and ancient prophecies...I found myself unable to put this book down till the end. Full of intrigue and suspense, it is a real page-turner. Excellently written...I highly recommend it."
    Book Review Cafe by
    Louise Riveiro-Mitchell
    (Author of *Autumn Sky*)

"A classic page-turner, without an excess of blood-spatters. There's plenty of action, but the suspense comes from McKenzie's efforts to outwit the shadowy figures who will stop at nothing to retrieve the scroll."
    Pat Browning, Author of *Full Circle*

"Secret of the Scroll attains its importance not in its storyline, but of the deft handling of the Israel-Palestine issue in the background of fiction. A good solid read...Recommended, a worthy read and an even more worthy buy.
    New Mystery Reader
    by Narayan Radhakrishman

"The author...produces an excellent thread of tension, which could snap at any time. We rated this book four hearts."
    Heartland Reviews by Bob Spear

"Spellbinding. Chester Campbell has crafted a real winner. Step into a forgotten cave and uncover a secret that can ignite a holy war...dig into this one and prepare to finish it in one sitting."
    Joyce Holland, Author of
    Beyond Gulf Breeze (a Sally
    Malone Mystery)

"This book does NOT let up on the action and tension and you MUST finish it to find out if anyone is getting out alive...you will NOT be able to put the book down til you finish it."

DorothyL review by
Linda Anderson

Check out these other fine titles by
Durban House at your local book store.

EXCEPTIONAL BOOKS
BY
EXCEPTIONAL WRITERS

FICTION

A DREAM ACROSS TIME	Annie Rogers
AFTER LIFE LIFE	Don Goldman
an-eye-for-an-eye.com	Dennis Powell
BASHA	John Hamilton Lewis
THE CORMORANT DOCUMENTS	Robert Middlemiss
CRISIS PENDING	Stephen Cornell
DANGER WITHIN	Mark Danielson
DEADLY ILLUMINATION	Serena Stier
DEATH OF A HEALER	Paul Henry Young
HANDS OF VENGEANCE	Richard Sand
HOUR OF THE WOLVES	Stephane Daimlen-Völs
A HOUSTON WEEKEND	Orville Palmer
JOHNNIE RAY & MISS KILGALLEN	Bonnie Hearn Hill & Larry Hill
THE LATERAL LINE	Robert Middlemiss
LETHAL CURE	Kurt Popke
THE MEDUSA STRAIN	Chris Holmes
MR. IRRELEVANT	Jerry Marshall
OPAL EYE DEVIL	John Hamilton Lewis
PRIVATE JUSTfCE	Richard Sand
ROADHOUSE BLUES	Baron Birtcher
RUBY TUESDAY	Baron Birtcher
SAMSARA	John Hamilton Lewis
SECRET OF THE SCROLL	Chester D. Campbell
SECRETS ARE ANONYMOUS	Fredrick L. Cullen
THE SEESAW SYNDROME	Michael Maddcn
THE SERIAL KILLER'S DIET BOOK	Kevin Mark Postupack

THE STREET OF FOUR WINDS	Andrew Lazarus
TUNNEL RUNNER	Richard Sand
WHAT GOES AROUND	Don Goldman

NONFICTION

BEHIND THE MOUNTAIN	Nick Williams
FISH HEADS, RICE, RICE WINE & WAR: A VIETNAM PARADOX	Lt. Col. Thomas G. Smith, Ret.
JIMMY CARTER AND THE RISE OF MILITANT ISLAM	Philip Pilevsky
MIDDLE ESSENCE- WOMEN OF WONDER YEARS	Landy Reed
SPORES, PLAGUES, AND HISTORY— THE STORY OF ANTHRAX	Chris Holmes
WHITE WITCH DOCTOR	Dr. John A. Hunt
PROTOCOL	Mary Jane McCaffree, Pauline Innis, and Richard Sand.

DURBAN HOUSE FICTION

A DREAM ACROSS TIME   Annie Rogers
   Jamie Elliott arrives from New York onto the Itish Caribbean island of St. Lucia, and finds herself caught tip in Island forces, powerful across the centuries, which Find deep echoes in her recurring dreams.

AFTER LIFE LIFE   Doti Goldman
   A hilarious murder mystery taking place in the afterlife. Andrew Law, Chief Justice of the Texas Supreme Court, is the picture of robust health when he suddenly dies. Upon arriving in the afterlife, Andy discovers he was murdered, and his untimely has death has soule some unexpected and far-reaching consequences—a worldwide depression, among others. Many diabolical plots are woven in this funny, fast-paced whodunit, with a surprising double-cross ending.

an-eye-for-an-eye.com   Dennis Powell
   Jed Warren, Vietnam Peacenik, and Jeff Porter, ex-Airborne, were close friends and executives at Megafirst Bank. So when CFO McAlister crashes the company, creams off millions in bonuses, and wipes out Jed and Jeff, things began to happen.

If you wonder about corporate greed recorded in today's newspapers, read what one man did about it in this intricate, devious, and surprise-ending thriller

BASHA — John Hamilton Lewis

LA reviewer, Jeff Krieder's pick as "Easily my best read of the year." Set in the world of elite professional tennis, and rooted in ancient Middle East hatreds of identity and blood loyalties, Basha is charged with the fiercely competitive nature of professional sports, and the dangers of terrorism. An already simmering Middle East begins to boil, and CIA Station Chief Grant Corbet must track down the highly successful terrorist, Basha. In a deadly race against time Grant hunts the elusive killer only to see his worst nightmare realized.

THE BEIRUT CONSPIRACY — John R. Childress

At some point every person is faced with a moral dilemma: the right choice or the easy choice. The Beirut Conspiracy is a fast-paced thriller torn from today's headlines. For newly elected US President Roswell Pierce, world peace or uncontrollable global terrorism wait his decision. For drunken and disbarred physician Matthew Richards, his time as a student in Beirut is about to catch up with him, forcing him into an equally difficult choice.

THE CORMORANT DOCUMENTS Robert Middlemiss

Who is Cormorant, and why is his coded letter on Hitler's stationary found on a WWI Nazi bomber preserved in the Arctic? And why is the plane loadedwith Goering's plundered art treasures? Mallory must find out or die. On the run front the British Secret Service and CIA, he finds himself caught in a secret that dates back to 1945.

CRISIS PENDING — Stephen Cornell

When U.S. oil refineries blow up, the White House and the Feds move fast, but not fast enough. Sherman Nassar Ramsey, terrorist for hire, a loner, brilliant, multilingual, and skilled with knives, pistols, and bare hands, moves around the country with contempt, case and cunning.

As America's fuel system starts grinding to a halt, rioting breaks out for gasoline, and food becomes scarce, events draw Lee Hamilton's wife, Mary, into the crisis. And when Ramsey kidnaps her, the battle becomes very personal.

DANGER WITHIN — Mark Danielson

Over 100 feet down in cold ocean waters lies the wreck of pilot Kevin Hamilton's DC-10. In it are secrets which someone is desperate to keep. When the Navy sends a team of divers from the Explosives Ordinance Division, a mysterious explosion from the wreck almost destroys the salvage ship. The FBI steps in with Special Agent Mike Pentaglia. Track the life and death of Global Express Flight 3217 inside the gritty world of aviation, and discover the shocking cargo that was hidden on its last flight.

DEADLY ILLUMINATION — Serena Stier

It's summer 1890 in New York City. A ebullient young woman, Florence Tod, must challenge financier, John Pierpont Morgan, to solve a possible murder. J.P's librarian has ingested poison embedded in an illumination of a unique Hildegard von Bingcn manuscript. Florence and her cousin, Isabella Stewart Gardner, discover the corpse. When Isabella secretly removes a gold tablet from the scene of the crime, she sets off a chain of events that will involve Florence and her in a dangerous conspiracy.

DESIGNED TO KILL — Chester D. Campbell

Award winning author Chester Campbell brings back Greg McKenzie and his wife, Jill, to the glistening white beaches at Perdido Key, Florida. Tim Gannon, son of the McKenzies's closest friends, has been found dead of a gunshot wound. 'Self-inflicted,' says the deputy who investigated, a clear case of remorse over the design flaw in a highrise beachfront condo that caused a balcony to collapse, killing two people. But, after two thugs work Greg over, he realizes Jill is in danger too, and if this is a murder case, he had better solve it fast.

HANDS OF VENGEANCE — Richard Sand

Private detective Lucas Rook returns still haunted by the murder of his twin brother. What seems like an easy case involving workplace violations, the former homicide detective finds himself locked in a life and death struggle with the deadly domestic terrorist group, The Brothers of the Half Moon. A must-read for lovers of dark mysteries.

HORIZON'S END — Andrew Lazarus

This wide-ranging international novel presents on man's long haunted pursuit of abandoned values on three continents—North America, Europe, and Asia. Through it all, the wartime sounds of Morse Code signals remind him of his journalist's mission to keep the faith and reveal the truth. Jack Lerner often finds himself in the arms of women who are brilliant, sultry, and enigmatic. He fights his fight facing tough decisions in honest news reporting and contending with a family's survival in a world that refuses to live up to his own personal moral standards.

HOUR OF THE WOLVES — Stephatic Daimlen-Völs

After more than three centuries, the Poisons Affair remains one of history's great, unsolved mysteries. The worst impulses of human nature—sordid sexual perversion, murderous intrigues, witchcraft, Satanic cults—thrive within the shadows of the Sun King's absolutism and will culminate in the darkest secret of his reign; the infamous Poisons Affair, a remarkably complex web of horror, masked by Baroque splendor, luxury and refinement.

A HOUSTON WEEKEND — Orville Palmer

Professor Edward Randall, not-yet-forty, divorced and separated from his daughters, is leading a solitary, cheerless existence in a university town. At a conference in Houston, he runs into his childhood sweetheart. Then she was poverty-stricken, American Indian. Now she's elegantly attired, driving an expensive Italian car and lives in a millionaires' enclave. Will their fortuitous encounter grow into anything meaningful?

THE INNOCENT NEVER KNEW   Mark W. Danielson

When Senator Sam Tinsdale's plane crashes short of the runway during a snowstorm and city-wide power failure, NTSB investigator is sent to Albuquerque to investigate. But when he arrives, he finds the crash site tampered with, evidence removed, and is threatened by men in snowsuits who refuse to provide I.D. When his boss, Ralph Dietz, issues a statement that the Cockpit Voice Recorder and Flight Data Recorder had failed, Stambler smells a cover-up.

JOHNNIE RAY AND MISS KILGALLEN   Bonnie Hearn Hill and Larry Hill

Based on the real-life love affair between 1950's singer Johnnie Ray and columnist Dorothy Kilgallen. They had everything—wealth, fame, celebrity. The last thing they needed was love. Johnnie Ray and Miss Kilgallen is a love story that travels at a dangerous, roaring speed. Driven close to death from their excesses, both try to regain their lives and careers in a novel that goes beyond the bounds of mere biography.

THE LAST COWBOYS   Robert E. Hollmann

What do you do when you have outlived your time?

Clint and Bubba, two aging cowboys, bodies worn out from rodeos and ranching, whose best days are behind them, try and survive in a citified world. Follow The Last Cowboys as they fight modern society in an attempt to hold on to the way of life they know and love.

THE LATERAL LINE   Robert Middlemiss

Kelly Travert was ready. She had the Israeli assassination pistol, she had coated the bullets with garlic, and tonight she would kill the woman agent who tortured and killed her father. When a negotiator for the CIA warns her, suddenly her father's death is not so simple anymore.

LETHAL CURE   Kurt Popke

Dr. Jake Prescott is a resident on duty in the emergency room when medics rush in with a double trauma involving patients sustaining injuries during a home invasion. Jake learns that one patient is the intruder, the other, his wife, Sara. He also learns that his four-year-old daughter, Kelly, is missing, and his patient may hold the key to her recovery.

THE MEDUSA STRAIN   Chris Holmes

Finalist for Fore Word Magazine's 'Book of the Year'. A gripping tale of bioterrorism that stunningly portrays the dangers of chemical warfare. Mohammed Ali

Ossman, a bitter Iraqi scientist who hates America, breeds a deadly form of anthrax, and develops a diabolical means to initiate an epidemic. It is a story of personal courage in the face of terror, and of lost love found.

MR. IRRELEVANT   Jerry Marshall

Booklist Star Review. Chesty Hake, the last man chosen in the NFL draft, has been dubbed Mr. Irrelevant. By every yardstick, he should not be playing pro football, but because of his heart and high threshold for pain, he endures. Then during his eighth and final season, he slides into paranoia, and football will never be the same.

NO ORDINARY TERROR   J. Brooks Van Dyke

In this elegant and meticulously researched Edwardian detective story, J. Brooks Van Dyke brings to life the stylized fashions and customs of the time, and weaves across them a story of treason, medicine, and murder. Follow Richard and Emma Watson, nephew and niece to the Watson of Sherlock Holmes fame, as they explore dangerous leads into aristocratic mansions and London's filthiest slums.

OPAL EYE DEVIL   John Hamilton Lewis

"Best historical thriller in decades." Good Books. In the age of the Robber Baron, Opal Eye Devil weaves an extraordinary tale about the brave men and women who risk everything as the discovery of oil rocks the world. The richness and pageantry of two great cultures, Great Britain and China, are brought together in a thrilling tale of adventure and human relationships.

PRIVATE JUSTICE   Richard Sand

Ben Franklin Award 'Best Mystery of the Year'. After taking brutal revenge for the murder of his twin brother, Lucas Rooks leaves the NYPD to become a private eye. A father turns to Rook to investigate the murder of his daughter. Rook's dark journey finds him racing to find the killer, who kills again and again as Private Justice careens toward a startling end.

ROADHOUSE BLUES   Baron R. Birtchcr

From the suii-drenched sands of Santa Catalina Island to the smoky night clubs and back alleys of West Hollywood, Roadhouse Blues is a taut noir thriller. Newly retired Homicide detective Mike Travis is torn from the comfort of his chartered yacht business into the dark, bizarre underbelly of Los Angeles's music scene by a grisly string of murders.

RUBY TUESDAY   Baron R. Birtcher

When Mike Travis sails into the tropical harbor of Kona, Hawaii, he expects to put LA Homicide behind him. Instead, he finds the sometimes seamy back streets and dark underbelly of a tropical paradise and the world of music and high finance, where wealth and greed are steeped in sex, vengeance, and murder.

SAMSARA — John Hamilton Lewis

A thrilling tale of love and violence set in post-World War Hong Kong. Nick Ridley, a captain in the RAF, is captured and sent to the infamous Japanese prisoner-of-war canip, Changi, in Singapore. He survives brutal treatment at the hands of the camp commandant, Colonel Tetsuro Matashima. Nick moves to Hong Kong, where he reunites with the love of his life, Courtney, and builds a world-class airline. On the eve of having his company recognized at the Crown Colony's official carrier, Courtney is kidnapped, and people begin to die. Nick is pulled into the quagmire, and must once again face the demon of Changi.

SECRET OF THE SCROLL — Chester D. Campbell

Finalist 'Deadly Dagger' award, and ForeWord Magazine's 'Book of the Year' award. Deadly groups of Palestinians and Israelis struggle to gain possession of an ancient parchment that was unknowingly smuggled from Israel to the U.S. by a retired Air Force investigator. Col. Greg McKenzie finds himself mired in the duplicitous world of Middle East politics when his wife is taken hostage in an effort to force the return of the first century Hebrew scroll.

SECRETS ARE ANONYMOUS — Frederick L. Cullen

A comic mystery with a cast of characters who weave multiple plots, puzzles, twists, and turns. A remarkable series of events unfold in the lives of a dozen residents of Bexley, Ohio. The journalism career of the principle character is derailed when her father shows up for her college graduation with his boyfriend on his way to a new life in California.

THE SEESAW SYNDROME — Michael Madden

A terrifying medical thriller that slices with a scalpel, exposing the greed and corruption that can happen when drug executives and medical researchers position thernselves for huge profits. Biosense Pharmaceuticals has produced a drug named Floragen, and now they need to test it on patients to gain FDA approval. But there's a problem with the new drug. One of the side effects included death.

THE SERIAL KILLER'S DIET BOOK — Kevin Postupack

Finalist ForeWord Magazine's 'Book of the Year' award. Fred Orbis is fat, but he dreams of being Frederico Orbisini, internationally known novelist, existential philosopher, raconteur, and lover of women. Both a satire and a reflection on morals, God and the Devil, beauty, literature, and the best-seller list, The Serial Killer's Diet Book is a delightful look at the universal human longing to become someone else.

THE STREET OF FOUR WINDS — Andrew Lazarus

Paris, just after World War II. A time for love, but also a time of political ferment. In the Left Bank section of the city, Tom Cortell, a tough, intellectual journalist, finally learns the meaning of love. Along with him is a gallery of fascinating characters who lead a merry and sometimes desperate chase between Paris, Switzerland, and Spain in search of themselves.

TAINTED ANGELS — Greg Crane
"One of the best mafia thrillers in years."
Tainted Angels tells the story of a Chicago crime family that defeats the Israeli underground's incursion into the New York drug market. After succeeding in New York, Mario Paterlini, with the help of his three sons, expand their narcotics empire in California, where he must deal with the CIA, Mexican drug lords, an Italian narcotics broker, and Los Angeles gangs.

TERMINAL CARE — Arvin Chawla
Billionaire Thomas Poole, Sr., does not believe his son died from an overdose. As he watches the life support being pulled from Michael's body, he wants vengeance, and not on any street-level punks. A fast, scary thriller that will make you think twice about that next hospital stay.

TUNNEL RUNNER — Richard Sand
A fast, deadly espionage thriller peopled with quirky and sometimes vicious characters, Tunnel Runner tells of a dark world where murder is committed and no one is brought to account, where loyalties exist side by side with lies and extreme violence.

WHAT GOES AROUND — Don Goldman
Finalist ForeWord Magazine's 'Book of the Year' award. Ray Banno, a medical researcher, was wrongfully incarcerated for bank fraud. What Goes Around is a dazzling tale of deception, treachery, revenge, and nonstop action that resolves around money, sex, and power. The book's sharp insight and hard-hitting style builds a high level of suspense as Banno strives for redemption.

DURBAN HOUSE NONFICTION

BEHIND THE MOUNTAIN: — Nick Williams
A CORPORATE SURVIVAL BOOK
A harrowing true story of courage and survival. Nick Williams is alone, and cut off in a blizzard bchind the mountain. In order to survive, Nick called upon his training and experience that made him a highly successful business executive. In Behind the Mountain: A Corporate Survival Book, you will find the finest practical advice on how to handle yourself in tough spots, be they life threatening to you, or threatening to your job performance or the company itself. Read and learn.

FISH HEADS, RICE, RICE WINE & WAR — LTC. Thomas G. Smith (Ret.)

A human, yet humorous, look at the strangest and most misunderstood war ever, in which American soldiers were committed. Readers are offered an insiders view ofAmerican life in the midst of highly deplorable conditions, which often lead to laughter.

JIMMY CARTER AND THE RISE OF MILITANT ISLAM — Philip Pilevsky

One of America's foremost authorities oil the Middle East, Philip Pilevsky argues that President Jimmy Carter's fallure to support the Shah of Iran led to the 1979 revolution. That revolution legitimized and provided a base ofoperations for militant Islamists across the Middle East. A most thought provoking book.

MIDDLE ESSENCE... WOMEN OF WONDER YEARS — Landy Reed

A wonderful book by renowned speaker Landy Reed that shows how real women in real circumstances have confronted and conquered the obstacles of midlife. This is a must have guide and companion to what can be the most significant and richest years of a woman's life.

PROTOCOL (25th Anniversary Edition) — Mary Jane McCaffree, Pauline Innis, and Richard Sand

Protocol is a comprehensive guide to proper diplomatic, official and social usage. The Bible for foreign governments, embassies, corporations, public relations firms, and individuals wishing to do business with the Federal Government. "A wealth of detail on every conceivable question, from titles and forms of address to ceremonies and flag etiquette." Department of State Newsletter.

SPORES, PLAGUES, HISTORY: THE STORY OF ANTHRAX — Chris Holmes

"Much more than the story of a microbe. It is the tale of history and prophecy woven into a fabric of what was, what might have been and what might yet be. What you are about to read is real—your are not in the Twilight Zone—adjusting your TV set will not change the picture. However, it is not hopeless, and we are not helpless. The same technology used to create biological weapons can protect us with better vaccines and . CDR Ted J. Robinson, U.S. Navy Epidemiologist.

WHAT MAKES A MARRIAGE WORK? — Malcolm D. Mahr

You hear the phrase "marry and settle down," which implies life becomes more serene and peaceful after marriage. This simply isn't so. Living together is one long series of experiments in accommodation. What Makes a Marriage Work? is a collection of fifty insights reflecting one couple's searching, experimenting, screaming, pouting, nagging, whining, moping, blaming, and other dysfunctional behaviors that helped them successfully navigate the turbulent sea of matrimony for over fifty years. (Featuring 34 New Yorker cartoons of wit and wisdom.)

WHITE WITCH DOCTOR   John A. Hunt
A true story of life and death, hope and despair in apartheid-ruled South Africa. White Witch Doctor details white surgeon John Hunt's fight to save his beloved country in a time of social unrest and political upheaval, drawing readers into the world of South African culture, mores and folkways, superstitions, and race relations.